**The embrace** so deliciously good, Hannah couldn't find it in herself to pull back.

The pressure of his strong hands around her waist, pulling her in close. The feel of his breath on her neck, all those touches that she had craved for so long, but denied herself for fear that it would just drive a deeper wedge between her and her brother.

But now, here, in the quiet of the vehicle, there was no way either of them could deny it. This sweetness between them, this need. She pressed her head into his shoulder, inhaling the scent of him and wondering how she had lasted so long without this.

When she pulled back slightly and looked into his eyes, she had no idea how he would feel. Would he push her off, tell her they couldn't do this? Or would he give her what she had needed for so long?

# PROTECTIVE REFUGE

## JANIE CROUCH

**H** Harlequin

**INTRIGUE**

**MIX**
Paper | Supporting responsible forestry
FSC® C021394
FSC www.fsc.org

To Denise...I couldn't tie my own shoe without you.
Thank you for making this series happen.

Recycling programs for this product may not exist in your area.

ISBN-13: 978-1-335-69061-6

Protective Refuge

Copyright © 2026 by Janie Crouch

For questions and comments about the quality of this book, please contact us at CustomerService@Harlequin.com.

TM and ® are trademarks of Harlequin Enterprises ULC.

Harlequin Enterprises ULC
22 Adelaide St. West, 41st Floor
Toronto, Ontario M5H 4E3, Canada
www.Harlequin.com

HarperCollins Publishers
Macken House, 39/40 Mayor Street Upper,
Dublin 1, D01 C9W8, Ireland
www.HarperCollins.com

**Printed in Lithuania**

**Janie Crouch** writes passionate romantic suspense for readers who still believe in heroes. After a lifetime on the East Coast—and a six-year stint in Germany—this *USA TODAY* bestselling author has settled into her dream home in the Front Range of the Colorado Rockies. She loves engaging in all sorts of adventures (triathlons! two-hundred-mile relay races! mountain treks!), traveling and surviving life with four kids. You can find out more about her at janiecrouch.com.

## Books by Janie Crouch

### Harlequin Intrigue

### *Warrior Peak Sanctuary*

*Protective Assignment*
*Protective Lawman*
*Protective Refuge*

### *San Antonio Security*

*Texas Bodyguard: Luke*
*Texas Bodyguard: Brax*
*Texas Bodyguard: Weston*
*Texas Bodyguard: Chance*

### *The Risk Series: A Bree and Tanner Thriller*

*Calculated Risk*
*Security Risk*
*Constant Risk*
*Risk Everything*

### *Omega Sector: Under Siege*

*Daddy Defender*
*Protector's Instinct*
*Cease Fire*

Visit the Author Profile page at Harlequin.com.

# CAST OF CHARACTERS

*Xavier Michaels*—Former CIA agent and co-owner of Warrior Peak Sanctuary. Runs the day-to-day operations of the center.

*Hannah Davies*—Longtime employee at Warrior Peak Sanctuary. Always ready to help with a friendly smile.

*Lawson Davies*—Former Army Special Forces and co-owner of Warrior Peak Sanctuary. Hannah's older brother and Xavier's best friend.

*Aaron Ward*—Former police officer who discovered corruption in his department and nearly lost everything because of it. Now works at Warrior Peak Sanctuary.

*Bailey Masters*—Police officer in Blue Ridge. Engaged to Aaron.

*Cade Thatcher*—Former soldier who now works at Warrior Peak Sanctuary and leads tactical missions there. Engaged to River.

*River Robertson*—Works at Warrior Peak Sanctuary as an assistant to the counselor. Engaged to Cade.

# *Chapter One*

"Get down!" Xavier Michaels roared to the rest of his team, gesturing for them to get behind the bullet-riddled truck that served as their only cover. The sound of gunshots filled the air, and his team—what remained of them, anyway—dove behind the truck after Xavier.

Xavier pressed his back to the vehicle, breath tearing from his lungs, and glanced over to Max, his younger brother, hunkered down behind the blown-out front wheel of the truck. He had that look on his face, the look that Xavier knew meant bad news.

Max rolled out from behind the truck and fired off a few shots, until his gun clicked uselessly—empty. No more ammunition around them. A couple of the other members of the group were scrambling to try to find cover, to no avail. Most of them were hit, carrying injuries, their blood mingling with the dust on the ground.

"Max!" Xavier called to his brother, and Max flashed him a grin. Xavier could hear the steady pulse of automatic weapons beyond them, and his own blood rushing in his ears. He didn't know what to do, but he had to keep his brother close.

Keeping his head down, Xavier crawled over to his brother, pulling him back behind the truck. He felt the

tension in his brother's body as he tried to keep him out
of the line of fire, but Max was already squirming away
from him, ready to get out of there.

"Listen to me," Xavier ordered his brother, and Max
finally turned to look at him, remembering that Xavier
was technically the one in charge here. They both ducked
as a bullet bounced with a metallic clang off the hood
of the truck, sending shrapnel spraying into the ground
around them.

"I have a few bullets left," he explained urgently, his
voice low. "And I'm going to use them to cover you. That
building, right there? You make a run for it and take cover
inside. I'll be out to meet you in no time, okay?"

"And then what?" Max shot back. "We're outnumbered. And you know backup isn't going to make it in
time."

Xavier's mind raced. He wanted to be able to argue
with his brother, but he knew he was right.

He could feel the situation quickly spinning out of
his control. He couldn't put his baby brother in harm's
way. He had promised their mother when they had both
left for the army that he would never do that. But the
way Max was staring out across the dusty ground before
them, spattered with bullets and blood, Xavier knew there
wasn't a chance he could stop his brother from what he
was about to do.

Max flashed him another grin. That devil-may-care
look that told Xavier he was ready to do whatever it took
to make it out. He had survived so much, and it had made
him cocky. There were only so many chances he had before his luck ran out.

"If this is how I have to go," he remarked, tightening his grip on his vest, "so be it. I had a good run."

"Max, you can't—"

But before Xavier could finish what he had to say, another spray of bullets rattled the truck. Xavier ducked, turning his back, and they skipped past him onto the ground below.

But when he turned back to his brother, he saw that he hadn't been so lucky.

A bloom of blood started to form around Max's throat, a wet darkness spreading out across his camouflage uniform. His eyes were hazy and distant, and Xavier's stomach dropped as he lurched toward him.

"Max!" he yelled. His hands reached out for his brother, but he couldn't get hold of him. He watched as his brother slipped away right before him, and he tried to scream his name again, but it did no good…

"Max!"

XAVIER CAME TO with a start, the sound of his own voice pulling him out of his nightmare. It took him a good thirty seconds to remind himself where he was. The memories were so vivid, the smell of blood and the sound of bullets so fresh in his mind, he couldn't seem to shake them.

But after a minute or so, he sank back into the bed and closed his eyes once more. He was in his room in the lodge at the Warrior Peak Sanctuary. It was the middle of the night, and silence filled the air around him. He wasn't at war; he wasn't fighting anyone. He was safe.

And yet the memory of that dream pressed heavily on his mind as he tried to come back down to earth. His body was still racked with tension, and his insides felt as though they had been shredded as he was forced to re-live the worst moment of his life for the hundredth time in the last few months.

When was it going to end? If it ever ended. Before the fire, the dreams had at least been a little more manage-able, but since the fire on the property outside the main lodge nearly three months before, it felt as though he had been tortured nonstop by these memories.

If there was one thing that always served to bring him back to real life, it was a freezing-cold shower—a tip he learned in basic training as a way to wake himself up for any particularly early morning missions. He didn't want to wake anyone up, wandering around the lodge at this hour, but he needed something to blast the memories of what had happened out of his mind, at least for a little longer.

Until he fell asleep again, of course.

He grabbed a change of clothes and made his way down to the showers. The whole place was quiet and peaceful. Normally, he would have enjoyed a little piece of silence, but right now, he could have used the company. Not that he would have made a point to talk about what was going on in his mind. No, running this place, people expected him to be strong.

People came here because they relied on him to handle himself and what he had been through. If they knew how tortured he really was, how much the guilt played on his mind and how much he had let his own brother down, they would never be able to trust him the same way.

He blasted the water on as cold as he could take it and stuck his hand beneath the shower head to try to ground himself. After stripping off his clothes, he stepped into the shower. His teeth started to chatter immediately as the cold seeped into his system.

He closed his eyes, but even with the cold water pounding on his back, he found his mind returning to the night of the fire. The way those flames had licked at the sky, the way it had felt like everything they had worked for was being ripped right out from underneath them. Sometimes, he wondered how they had made it through without any major injuries. Things had looked so bleak at the time; he had accepted in the back of his mind the possibility that the main lodge might go up in smoke with the paddock and surrounding grounds.

But Lawson would never have let that happen. They had both worked too hard to get to this point, to create a sanctuary for people like them who needed a chance to get their feet back under them. They weren't going to let something like a fire change that.

Plenty of people didn't like what they were doing here, but that wasn't his problem. No, he just had to focus on keeping the place open and doing everything he could to protect those who trusted him enough to stay here.

He wasn't sure how long he stayed in that shower. But by the time he stepped out, the cold had soaked all the way through to his bones and his mind felt a little bit clearer. He knew there were probably better, more comfortable ways of dealing with these dreams than ice-cold showers, but the showers worked just fine for him in a pinch.

Maybe it would be smart to utilize some of the therapy they offered to their guests, but he had too much to do to spend his time talking about his feelings. Plus, again, what would everyone think of him? The lodge still needed some fixing up, even though it had been months since the fire, and he felt like it would be a long time before it was truly back to the way he wanted it.

Making his way back up the corridor toward his room, he found himself slowing, not wanting to be alone in there again. Instead of a place to rest and rejuvenate, his bedroom had become a place of torment these last few months with the nightmares that filled his head whenever he closed his eyes.

Even though it had been years since he lost his brother, the memories of that day still bled into his mind all the time. That last look Max had given him, the way he had told him that he was happy going out this way… Had he meant it?

Xavier had to believe he did. Because the alternative was too horrible to imagine.

He reached his bedroom door once more and was immediately struck by how cold it was. Not just the cold he was carrying in from the shower but something else—something that jumped out to him at once. He tensed, looking around, his instincts telling him something was wrong.

Inside the room, he took in anything that had changed since he was last there.

The curtains had been pulled back. The window had been thrown open, letting in a rush of the freezing mountain air. No way would Xavier have left it that way himself. He never slept with the curtains or the window open. It was way too dangerous to open yourself up to an enemy like that, especially when you were in such a vulnerable state as sleeping.

But he flicked on the light and saw more out of place.

The dresser drawers had all been pulled open, and it

looked as though his clothes had been rummaged through. He widened his eyes, making his way toward the piece of furniture cautiously, as though it might have been rigged with something. He rooted through his belongings, trying to see if there was anything missing, but nothing jumped out at him.

He had left the door unlocked when he went for his shower. A mistake on his part—but he had no reason to think he couldn't trust everyone in this lodge. Unless there was someone here who meant trouble, someone they hadn't done enough research into, someone who was going to cause problems down the line.

Whoever had been in here, they hadn't just been going through his stuff for no reason. No, the way the room had been turned over, they had been looking for something. Searching for something specific. But what?

He couldn't see anything missing, and it wasn't as though he kept anything of importance in his room anyway. Unless they counted the small handful of family memorabilia he kept on his bedside table, pictures of him and Max and their parents.

But just because he didn't think there was anything worth taking in here didn't mean everyone else agreed. Someone had to have been keeping a close eye on the place to know when he had left his room, and they had pounced on the opportunity to get in there and search through all of his stuff.

He closed his dresser drawers, then pushed the window back into place and locked it. Then, he scanned the dark grounds outside, checking to see if there was anything that looked suspicious before pulling the curtains shut again. Not that he thought whoever did this would hang around long enough to be seen.

There was nothing but the sound of crickets in the air, and stillness that suddenly seemed eerie knowing there was trouble afoot.

Whatever it was, he would get to the bottom of it, Xavier promised himself. He always did.

And this time would be no exception.

## Chapter Two

Hannah Davies wandered away from the lodge, the scent of maple syrup still fresh in her senses after cleaning up from the breakfast crowd in the cafeteria. Part of her morning routine after eating her first meal of the day was to go out for a walk around the property. She used it as time to clear her head and ready herself for her daily duties and to see how the seasons were changing at the place she had come to call home.

It was a cold, crisp February morning as she made her way down the path toward the cabins in the forested area. Along the edge of the path were the flowerbeds she had planted before the first frost back in the fall. It was going to be a few more months before she saw them come to fruition, but she could hardly wait for the explosion of color and scent her tulips and peonies were going to bring. Lawson, her brother, had tried to tell her there was no point putting so much energy into the flowers here, but she knew he was going to see why she had done it when they all started to bloom. This place could use a little color after the fire, and she was glad to be the one to make that happen.

She could still hear the buzz of activity inside the lodge as everyone went about getting settled into their daily routine. Hannah would be at the front desk for the rest of the day, which was why she was so intent on stretching her legs and clearing her mind for a while. If there was one thing she had learned in her time here, it was that it didn't suit her to be cooped up all day. With the beautiful scenery just a few feet from the door, she had no excuse not to get out into nature for at least a few minutes every day.

Tipping her head back, she paused as she reached the small cluster of cabins at the end of the path. Inhaling a deep lungful of air, she let the chill rush through her. Nothing cleared her head like the cold. She loved the summer, of course she did, with all the brightness of life around her, but there was no doubt she was going to miss these cold mornings when they passed.

Suddenly, a noise caught her attention—a laugh. She glanced around and quickly located the source coming from the newest cabin that had been built over the last few months. Through the large front window, she saw Bailey laughing as Aaron playfully chased her.

Hannah smiled. She was so happy for the two of them and that they had found each other once more. Every time she saw them together, it was clear they had been made for one another. Anyone could tell how much they loved each other. It was obvious in their actions and written all over their faces whenever they were together.

A little pang of jealousy twisted in her chest, but she tried her best to ignore it. She wasn't going to let her own lack of luck in love stop her from being happy for her friends. That was what this place was for, right? A chance for people to make a new start and discover their own calling in life. And for these two, that calling was with one another, taking care of each other and supporting each other through whatever life threw at them. And life had thrown a lot at them over the past several months.

Turning her back to give them some privacy, Hannah was about to head back up to the lodge when she caught sight of someone else making their way up the path toward the cabins. A familiar figure, hands stuffed in his pockets, eyes downcast, about thirty feet away.

She bit her lip and smiled, then lifted her hand to greet him. "Hey, Xavier!"

He didn't seem to notice her.

She frowned. It wasn't windy or raining. There was no reason he wouldn't have heard her. She called to him again, but he still didn't seem to hear. Finally, when she got closer and lifted her voice a little, his head snapped up, and he seemed almost startled to see her.

"Oh hey, Hannah," he greeted as he closed the distance between them.

She frowned again. What was wrong? Something was clearly bothering him. He always paid attention to his surroundings and wasn't usually quite so somber.

"You okay?" she asked.

He ran a hand over his short cropped dark hair, his hazel eyes darkening slightly as he frowned. But then he nodded firmly, clearly deciding against telling her what he was so deep in thought about. "Yeah, I'm fine."

She could tell he was lying. Maybe if she gave him a little encouragement, he would be more willing to share. "Didn't see you at breakfast," she remarked, trying to keep her voice casual. "You don't normally miss pancakes."

"Guess I must have overslept," he replied with a shrug.

"That's not like you," she pointed out. "Military man, you always keep good time, right?"

He managed a smile. His eyes creased as he looked down at her, and she felt an all-too-familiar flip in her chest. God, she needed to do something about that. She should have known better by now than to let the chemistry between them mess with her head. One kiss all those months ago should have been enough to get it out of her system, and yet, here she was, just as fluttery as she had always been about her brother's best friend.

"I try," he replied, and he glanced around. "What are you doing out here this morning anyway? It's freezing."

"I like the cold," she told him. "Helps clear my head."

"I get that," he said.

They were dancing around the real point here. She could feel that in her bones. But she didn't know how to nudge him along to what was really on his mind. There were dark circles beneath his eyes—it was obvious he hadn't been sleeping much. But what had been keeping him up?

Maybe she was overthinking it. Ever since the night of the fire, she had been more nervous than ever before, worried that something might disrupt the comfortable peace she had found at the lodge.

She shifted a little closer to him, looking up into his eyes. For a split second, she felt it, the same draw that had led to their impromptu kiss last year. She had done everything she could to keep that out of her mind, to force herself to forget about how good his lips had felt on hers, but it wasn't that easy. No matter how much she tried to shut it off, the long-standing crush she had on him just wouldn't go away. Even knowing her brother hated the thought of his baby sister and his best friend together.

He was just protective of both of them.

"Is something going on?" she pressed.

He paused for a second, as though he was really considering telling her the truth. But then, he withdrew once more. Shaking his head, he glanced back toward the main building. "Nothing," he said at last. "I should get to work for the day. See you around, Hannah."

And with that he was gone.

She watched as he went and thought about calling after him once more. Begging him to tell her what was troubling him. She parted her lips, about to call his name, then stopped herself. His business and troubles were his own, even if she wished for something different. He had made it clear where he stood after their kiss all those months ago, and the last thing she needed was to make things more complicated than she already had.

Her shoulders slumped as she stood there, trying to calm the pounding of her heart. How was it that he could still have this effect on her even after all this time? She had felt it the moment she met him so many years ago when he served in the military with her brother. What had started as a simple crush had developed into something way more prominent.

He never seemed to return the feelings, always keeping her at a distance. And then after the moment they'd shared, she was more confused than ever. Even though she had started it, when their lips touched, he immediately took over—like he'd been waiting for the chance—and all but devoured her. But then suddenly it was over, and it felt like there was more distance between them than ever.

Even though she had tried to forget, she found herself thinking about it all the time. What it would be like to be with him and kiss him anytime she wanted, not having to worry about what someone else thought, especially her brother?

She could still remember the way Lawson had flipped his lid about it, as though he hadn't noticed the tension between them. Maybe he really hadn't, and all of this had come as a complete shock to him. But everyone else seemed to be able to tell how much chemistry she and Xavier had. Was her brother really that clueless?

It didn't matter. He had made himself clear. He didn't want anything happening between his best friend and his sister, and she supposed she couldn't blame him. What guy would be all right with his business partner and closest friend making a move on his little sister?

Lawson had always been way more protective of Hannah than he needed to be. No matter how much she tried to convince him that she was perfectly capable of taking care of herself, he would brush her off and act like she needed someone looking out for her. It was frustrating sometimes, but hey, he was her big brother. It wasn't as though she could expect anything else—it had been that way her entire life.

She watched from a distance and waited for Xavier to make it back to the lodge before she started walking again. She didn't want him to feel like she was following him or chasing him around. God knew she had done enough of that as it was.

Sometimes, she wished she could just ask him where his feelings for her stood. Surely, her brother's attitude hadn't been enough to shut down everything Xavier felt for her. Would it? She didn't know. And with no way to ask him without giving away her own lingering emotions, she had decided it was best to just keep it all to herself.

Another explosion of laughter burst from the cabin closest to her, and this time the sound of River and Cade's flirtation echoed down the pathway. Hannah knew she wasn't going to get far being envious of the other women around here, but damn, sometimes she wondered when it was going to be her turn to fall for someone and have them want her back.

She couldn't fault either couple for their happiness, either. All four of her friends had been through some hard times and she was grateful they'd all made it beyond their troubles to find contentment together at Warrior Peak.

She remembered back when Cade first showed up with his own healing to do and had River in tow. He'd spotted her hitchhiking at night in the rain and brought her up to the lodge unaware of the trouble following her. Then Aaron had shown up fighting his own demons and took the job as the sanctuary's handyman. He kept to himself until Bailey showed up looking for him with bad people on her trail.

Yeah, they'd all been through some trouble, but had fought their battles hard and won, and even come out the other side stronger together.

That was what she wanted. Not the battles and dangers, per se, but the deep connection, the strength and unity. Being together with that one person who wanted you back with the same fierceness.

Her time would come. She had to tell herself that. She had done her best to stay optimistic, but sometimes, it felt like none of this was really fair. She didn't know how much longer she would have to wait—and if the man she was meant to be with was already right there in front of her.

But Xavier was her brother's best friend and had been part of their lives forever. She knew it would make everything crazy-complicated if the two of them got involved. Plus, they worked together, too. Wasn't that a cardinal sin, dating someone you worked with? God, it was all so complicated, Hannah didn't know where to start.

Maybe a little more time out here in the cold would do her good. She decided to head a little farther into the forest, hoping the canopy of trees around her would give her some space to think.

The look on Xavier's face told her there was more going on with him than she knew about. And she wasn't sure exactly what to think about that. After the fire, she was uneasy in a way she hadn't been before, and any little thing that seemed off was enough to get her mind spinning.

Especially when it came from the man she couldn't get out of her head.

# *Chapter Three*

Xavier stepped back inside the lodge, rubbing his hands together as the warmth of the crackling fire in the reception area rushed through his body. It had been Hannah's idea to put it in, to create a warmer and cozier ambience for those first arriving at the lodge, and it had been a great addition. Every time he saw it, he felt a little more relaxed. God only knew how much he needed that right now.

His stomach grumbled as he headed down to the kitchen. He had skipped out on breakfast, oversleeping after he had been up in the middle of the night. Even when he fell back into a fitful sleep after his cold shower, the dreams had plagued him enough that he hadn't been able to get any real rest, no matter how hard he tried. Now, he could feel the weight of that lack of sleep pressing down on his shoulders. He hoped it wasn't too obvious.

Though, judging by the way Hannah had looked at him when he ran into her outside, he wasn't doing a good job keeping it to himself. He didn't want to worry anyone, but at the same time, there was only so long he could wait this out before he had to admit defeat and get help.

Arriving at the kitchen, he found Sarah Peterson, Warrior Peak's counselor, finishing up with the dishes.

She flashed him a grin. "All the pancakes are gone,"

she told him. "But there's some bacon and eggs left on the stove if you want something."

"Thanks, Sarah," he replied, and he went to help himself to a hearty breakfast, even if he really didn't feel much like it. His stomach twisted into knots as he thought about what he had come back to the night before. He still had no explanation for what had happened to his room, and that bothered him. He liked everything in his world to be in order, everything in its place. That was how he handled the stress of everything he had been through, how he survived in the mess of the life he'd led so far. But someone tossing his room was something he hadn't been ready for, and he didn't like the way it made him feel.

"You need a hand with those?" he asked Sarah, nodding to the dishes she was working through.

She waved a hand. "I'm fine," she replied. "Hannah already brought everything in from the dining area, and I'm just finishing up. You have something to eat."

He nodded at her gratefully and went to take a seat in the empty dining hall. The smell of pancakes and maple syrup lingered in the air, a reminder of what he had missed. Even if he had been awake, he doubted he would have bothered coming down here to join everyone. He wouldn't have been in the mood to put himself in a roomful of people who might guess something was up.

He didn't want questions, he didn't want interrogation, and he didn't want anyone to know what was really going on inside his head. He'd needed the cool morning walk and space to clear his head a little more and think. Someone there at the lodge, after all, had likely been the one to go through his room in the middle of the night. If that was the case, he didn't want to give them any indication that he was on to them.

He knew from his CIA days that playing it cool was the best way to get a rat out of hiding, and he intended to smoke out this person one way or another.

Just as Xavier was finishing his food, Lawson appeared in the doorway. Xavier caught his friend's eye, and as soon as he did, his stomach dropped. Lawson's mouth was set into a hard line, and judging by the look on his face, Xavier could tell he wanted to have a serious conversation.

Xavier sighed and set aside his plate as Lawson came to join him, sliding in to the long wooden bench that ran along the other side of the communal table.

"Didn't see you at breakfast today," Lawson stated.

Xavier had hoped his absence wouldn't be that obvious, but looked like he hadn't gotten so lucky. He shrugged and tried to keep his voice steady. "Overslept."

Lawson paused, giving Xavier a chance to share more, but when he didn't, he sighed and cocked his head at him. "I know something's going on with you," he said bluntly.

Leave it to Lawson to jump right to the heart of the matter. His friend had never been one to mince his words, but Xavier's back was instantly up. Did he know something about the room invasion last night? "What are you talking about?" Xavier fired back. He knew Lawson was on his side, but there was a part of him that didn't like letting anyone in. After everything he'd been through in his life, he felt like he needed to be on his guard at all times, even around his best friend.

"The nightmares are back, aren't they?" Lawson pressed.

Xavier looked down at the table. He didn't need to reply. Lawson had been there with him when Xavier was first navigating the nightmare of surviving his brother's loss. Lawson had seen how much it tore Xavier apart. Xavier wished he had some way to deny it, but there would have been no point. Lawson knew him better than anyone else in the world.

"You've been off ever since the fire," Lawson continued, raising his eyebrows pointedly. "You don't need to hide it from me, man. I remember—"

"It's fine," Xavier cut him off before he could go any further. He didn't want to get into it, not now. There were other, more important things to think about. He wasn't going to dwell on the memories that he had worked so hard to leave in the past. Even if his brain didn't agree while he was sleeping.

Lawson grimaced. "Healing isn't linear," he reminded him. "God knows you've learned that just like I have, seeing what people go through here. There's no shame in needing help. That's what we have Sarah for—"

Xavier shook his head again. He knew Lawson was just trying to help, but that was the last thing on earth he needed right now. His best friend was trying to look out for him, but the thought of dredging up all those old memories once more made his chest hurt. He wasn't going to put himself through that. Not a chance in hell. "I'm fine," Xavier insisted, brushing him off.

"I saw how bad it got last time," Lawson reminded him, dropping his voice slightly.

Xavier straightened up, rolling his shoulders back and trying to figure out the best way to get his friend off his case. "Someone was in my room last night."

Lawson stared at him for a moment, frowning at the sudden change of subject. Then he blinked and blinked again like he was trying to process the information. "What are you talking about?"

"I went down to the showers in the middle of the night," Xavier explained, skipping the part where he'd been woken up by a nightmare. "When I got back, the window to my room was open, and someone had been through all my drawers."

Lawson's eyebrows rose. "Was anything missing?"

"Not that I could see," Xavier replied. "I'll have another look today, now that I'm all the way awake, but it didn't seem like anything had been taken."

"Damn," Lawson muttered, shaking his head. "Who do you think it was? Got any ideas?"

"None," Xavier admitted. "I don't know anyone here who would want to go through my stuff like that."

"You have any idea what they were looking for?"

"Not like I've got anything worth taking," Xavier pointed out with a shrug. "But if I figure it out, I'll let you know."

"Who could have got in like that?" Lawson wondered out loud. His voice turned hard and tense, the prior conversation forgotten.

Much to Xavier's relief. "I don't know. If I'm being generous, I might have said it was just someone sleepwalking, but…"

He trailed off. There was nothing else they needed to say, not really. After the fire, everyone at Warrior Peak had been unsettled. They couldn't let their guard down, and they had to assume everything was a threat after what had happened. The attack on the sanctuary grounds had underlined just how vulnerable this place was. With the doors open to anyone who needed it, it was difficult to track who might have been here for reasons other than the right ones.

"You keep your doors locked and your head up," Lawson told him. "I'll have a look through the security footage around the area. I know we don't have any cameras in the rooms or inner hallways specifically, but we might be able to catch someone sneaking around in the outer hallways and doors and the common areas. Maybe they didn't realize they were being recorded."

"Thanks," Xavier replied. "Let me take a look at it, too. I want to know who was poking around in my room."

Lawson nodded, then stood like the conversation was over.

Xavier got to his feet as well, grabbing his dishes to take them back to the kitchen. He was glad he had managed to deflect the more serious conversation before they got too deep into it. He didn't want to have to flesh out the details of his bad dreams to Lawson. They were just dreams, after all. Of course they sucked, but other than messing with his sleep, which made him tired the next day, they didn't have an impact on his real life. No matter how real they seemed in the moment.

"You better wash that up or the women will have your head," Lawson joked, walking toward the kitchen.

Xavier grinned and headed over to the sink to start taking care of his dishes. He knew Lawson was right. Sarah and Hannah were sticklers for cleanliness, always making sure the kitchen, dining hall, and other common areas were as clean as possible with so many different people always around. He wasn't going to be the idiot who left a dirty plate out under their watchful eyes.

He turned on the water and let it run until it was warm. Though most of the lodge building had been refitted, the pipes still took time to get going once the water was turned on, especially in the colder weather, rattling and groaning in the walls. And even more so with multiple people in the showers at the same time. It turned into a clinking and clanking symphony of sounds.

But that was why he liked this place so much. Even after all these years and all these changes, it still held some memories of what it had been in the first place, a rustic retreat built for a family to escape to. They had managed to build on that legacy, turning it into a new safe space for all the people who needed one.

He didn't even know the extent of everything the guests here had been through, but he didn't have to. He could see it written all over their faces, the tension and drawn expressions when they first arrived, and then the slow unfurling of their true personalities and potential the longer they stayed and the more they healed. It was an honor to bear witness to the healing and growth that happened at Warrior Peak.

Maybe he was a hypocrite for not doing the same, but he couldn't find it in him to want to heal right now.

Lawson leaned in the doorway, and Xavier could feel his eyes on him. Xavier glanced over at him, raising his eyebrows as though nudging him to say whatever was on his mind.

"Just think about it, man," Lawson told Xavier, coming over to slap him on the shoulder. "Sarah's here to help people. What you're going through, it's exactly her realm of expertise. You should consider it, at least."

Xavier sighed. He knew Lawson wasn't going to let this go until he had at least agreed to that. He nodded. "Sure, I'll consider it."

"Good," Lawson replied and headed for the door.

As he left, Xavier realized that he had let the water run until it was far too hot, and his hand was nearly scalding beneath the flow. He drew it back quickly, sucking in a sharp breath, and put on the cold tap to try to even it out.

Staring down at the dishes before him, his mind drifted back to his room, ransacked and rummaged through. That was the most important thing to get to the bottom of right now, not his nightmares and why they were so frequent again after the fire. There was someone, maybe even someone staying at the lodge, who was causing trouble, and he wasn't going to let them get away with it.

This place was his home, and these people were his family. He was going to protect them at all costs.

# Chapter Four

Hannah wrapped her hands around her hot chocolate, the last of which was swirling in the bottom of her mug, as she glanced out into the darkness and tried to muster the courage to go outside and head back to her cabin.

"I don't think I'll ever get used to this kind of cold," Bailey complained as the two women sat in the small common room toward the back of the lodge.

Hannah chuckled. "Oh trust me, you're not going to have much of a choice," she teased.

Bailey rolled her eyes. "I have no idea how I'm going to survive," she announced, laying the back of her hand on her forehead in a dramatic swoon.

"At least you have Aaron to keep you warm," Hannah pointed out without thinking.

Bailey cocked an eyebrow. "You think it'd be easier for you if you had a guy waiting back at your cabin for you?"

Hannah shrugged, feeling her cheeks start to get a little warm. "I don't know," she muttered. She didn't want to admit how lonely she'd been feeling these last few months. More than ever she found herself wishing for companionship like River and Bailey had with their men.

Both women had fought hard for their relationships, and deserve every moment of happiness they had. Bailey against the crooked cops she and Aaron had to expose to find their second chance and River and Cade dealing with River's past, including an obsessed cult leader. They'd all faced devastating odds and had come out the other side stronger and more settled as couples in loving relationships. Hannah longed to have what her friends had.

Someone to stay in and cuddle with on the dark, freezing winter nights. Someone to share the day's troubles and setbacks. Sometimes, she would lie in bed and stare out into the cold night beyond, wondering how she was supposed to get through another year without someone by her side.

It felt like everyone around her was settling down and getting comfortable in a life with someone else, but she was still in her cabin alone. She didn't want to go back to it, not quite yet, not when this hot chocolate and company was so cozy.

"Well, I guess I should get back to my cabin. Aaron will be wondering what happened to me," Bailey announced, getting to her feet and stretching. "You ready to brave the cold with me, Hannah?"

"Guess I could give it a shot," Hannah agreed, standing.

But before they could make it anywhere, the lights cut out.

"Oh no," Bailey muttered in the sudden darkness. "What's going on?"

Hannah pulled her phone out and switched on the flashlight so the two of them could avoid bumping into furniture while the back-up generators kicked into action. It wasn't entirely unusual for things to go wrong around here, especially in the winter. The cold weather sometimes froze the pipes and made it difficult for repairmen to get out as quickly as they might have normally.

But as they stood there, nothing happened. The beam of Hannah's phone light cut through the darkness, but no other lights were clicking back on.

"Shouldn't the backup generators have kicked in by now?" Hannah asked, a little nervous. She suddenly felt like the darkness was consuming them. Her mind couldn't help flashing back to the fire a few months earlier, like it did every time lately when something went wrong. Something like this was enough to make her palms sweat and her heart beat out of her chest.

"I think so," Bailey muttered. "Come on, let's get out to the front. The fireplace will give us some light, at least."

Hannah let Bailey lead the way but kept her phone flashlight trained in front of them as the two women made their way to the reception area of the lodge. The fire crackled cozily when they got there, but the usual comforting aura of the flames in the hearth didn't do much to settle Hannah's nerves.

"I swear," a voice cut through the darkness, two sets of footsteps coming toward them, "if the power in this place has gone down after I paid all that money to set up new generators, I'm going to kick some serious a—"

"It's going to be okay," Xavier soothed Lawson, and Hannah felt calm wash over her as soon as she heard his voice. Even after everything that had happened between them, she found his presence enormously comforting. As long as he was around, she knew they would figure out what was going on somehow.

"You know what's happening?" Bailey asked Lawson and Xavier as they reached the women.

Lawson shook his head, lit by the glow of a flashlight in his hand. "No idea. I just got those generators for the winter, so they should have kicked on by now. Xavier and I are going to go out and check what's going on."

"I'll come with you," Hannah replied at once, without thinking. Her brother pulled a face, clearly trying to think of some way he could talk her out of it, but Xavier nodded in agreement.

"We could use as many eyes on it as possible," Xavier agreed. "Bailey, you want to come, too?"

"I think I could brave the cold," Bailey replied. "Plus, I really don't want to stay in here alone." She put on the coat she'd been carrying. Hannah did the same, and they followed the guys out to the generators at the far side of the lodge.

It was bitingly cold outside, and the freezing air nipped at Hannah's skin. She moved to zip her coat up, but with her phone in one hand she couldn't get a proper grip on the zipper. She turned off her phone's flashlight, intent on putting it in her pocket, but with the light off, it was too dark to see the ground in front of her. Suddenly, her shoe snagged in a crack in the sidewalk, and she tripped.

"Ahh!" she yelled and fell to her knees.

Everyone spun around to make sure she was all right, but she had already hit the ground with a painful thump, scratching up her knees in the process.

"Hannah, are you okay?" Xavier asked as he rushed over. Crouching down, he put his arm around her, and the feel of his warm touch on her made her head spin.

"Uh, I'm fine," she managed, glad he couldn't see the flush to her cheeks or just how much she enjoyed having him so close to her. He helped her up, and she leaned on him a little longer than necessary.

Lawson chose that moment to sweep his flashlight over her, to make sure she was okay, and Hannah had to lower her gaze to the ground to avoid being blinded by the light in her eyes. She hoped he hadn't noticed the dreamy look on her face while she leaned into Xavier, enjoying his comfort and warmth.

"Someone must have cut the power on purpose," Xavier growled, his arm still around Hannah holding her to his side. It didn't strictly need to be there, but there was no way she was going to be the one to pull back.

Bailey shot her a pointed look in the flashlight's glow, as though she could sense the tension between them too, and Hannah bit into her lip and quickly lowered her gaze again. She hoped the other woman wouldn't say anything in front of Lawson. As far as her brother knew, there was nothing left between her and Xavier at all. The last thing she needed at a time like this was Lawson getting mad. They had other things to focus on.

"And it's getting people hurt," Xavier added, squeezing Hannah's shoulder slightly.

Hannah's pulse fluttered, hearing the protectiveness in his voice, as if he wanted to do everything he could to look out for her.

"I just scuffed up my knees, that's all. I'm okay, really," Hannah replied. "Let's go out to the generators and see if there's anything we can find."

Xavier finally let go of Hannah, and she immediately missed his warmth.

The group continued along the path to the generators without any further injuries. When they got there, sure enough, lengths of wire had been yanked out of the control panels and snipped. It looked neat and precise, as though someone had come with the tools to make it happen and knew what they were doing.

Lawson grabbed the wires, inspecting them closely. "Who the hell would have done this?" he demanded to nobody in particular, turning back around to face the group.

"The Haynes brothers, I bet," Bailey cut in.

Hannah turned to Bailey with a groan. "The guys who live at the ranch just over the mountain?"

"Yeah, them," Bailey replied. "They'd be my first suspects anyway."

"But why would they have done this?" Hannah asked, confused. She didn't exactly have many good things to say about the brothers, but she doubted they would have gotten involved in something like this.

"I don't know," Bailey replied. "To cause trouble."

Lawson and Xavier exchanged a look.

All of a sudden, Hannah felt a familiar feeling deep down in her stomach—a feeling she had promised herself she would never ignore again. It was the same feeling she'd had on the night of the fire, just before she had smelled the smoke filling the air and been faced with the cruel reality of what was happening.

She wrapped her arms around herself. "I want to go back inside."

Bailey nodded. "Come on, let's go," she agreed, taking Hannah's arm and steering her back down the walkway toward the main doors. "I'll take a look at those knees for you."

Hannah was more careful about where she stepped this time. Sneaking a look at Bailey out of the corner of her eye, she tried to ask her next question as carefully as she could. Bailey was a police officer down in Blue Ridge and she didn't want to cause problems or get the other woman in trouble by asking too many questions. "Why do you think the Haynes brothers might have had something to do with this?" she asked. "They've pestered us on and off in the past but it's never been anything that's caused real damage. Is there something official going on with them in town?"

"Because they live nearby and like to cause trouble, and I've seen plenty of reports at the police station coming in about them over the last few months." Bailey sighed. "Nothing too serious, mostly just intimidation around town, but they've clearly gotten it into their heads that they have some kind of ownership of the lodge. They've been heard mouthing off to whoever will listen when they've been drinking. I don't know how far that might go."

Hannah shivered. Her only encounter with the Haynes brothers had been when the younger one, Ron, had cat-called her in town. And then he had followed her almost halfway back up the mountain to Warrior Peak before he gave up. It had spooked her, sure, but she had just chalked it up to a bad experience and figured they would leave it there.

"That definitely is unsettling. But I still don't understand why they would want to cause trouble here? I mean, are they targeting this place or Lawson and Xavier specifically?" Hannah wondered aloud as they entered the lodge once more. The two women paused in front of the fire, turning their hands back and forth in front of the flames to warm themselves through.

"Honestly, I don't know," Bailey admitted. "They were

just my first thought with all the other complaints about disturbances by them in the area.

"Do you think they know about Lawson's and Xavier's backgrounds?" Hannah asked. "I mean, it seems kind of crazy to start something with both being former military and CIA."

"Yeah, but the Haynes brothers have never struck me much as guys with any smarts," Bailey pointed out. "There might be a reason they're doing all this now. Maybe I'll go around to their ranch with Sheriff Willis tomorrow, see if I can figure out what they're doing."

"You don't think that might aggravate them?" Hannah asked nervously. She didn't like the thought of Bailey getting into trouble, though she knew Bailey could handle it a million times better than she would ever have been able to.

"It might," Bailey admitted. "But I can't just stand aside and let them do whatever they want to this place. Warrior Peak is sacred ground as far as I'm concerned."

Hannah smiled. She was right about that. The lodge and the core staff here were a safe place for Hannah, had been for years now. She loved it up here, even if it was cut off from the rest of the world. She had everything she needed, and she wouldn't ask for a thing more than that.

Apart from the Haynes brothers, if they really were behind this, to leave them the hell alone, of course.

The sound of a car drew their attention, and both women lifted their heads. A pair of taillights were vanishing out of sight, and Hannah knew from a glance who they belonged to.

Uh-oh. Looked like Xavier was going to confront the Haynes brothers all on his own.

Hannah didn't envy them one bit.

# *Chapter Five*

Xavier drummed his fingers on the wheel, his teeth gritted as Lawson stared out the passenger window.

"They can't keep getting away with this," Lawson stated suddenly. "All the problems they've been causing around town have gone on for way too long. It has got to stop."

Lawson had agreed with Xavier the moment he suggested they go to the Haynes' ranch and talk to them face-to-face. Might not have been a good idea, since they didn't exactly have hard proof that the brothers had been the ones to vandalize the generators at the lodge, but they had been causing enough trouble these last few months to at least warrant a visit.

The Haynes brothers, Ron and Dave, were making waves in the small town of Blue Ridge, North Carolina, every time Xavier turned around—or at least, that was what it felt like. Whether it was squaring up to someone at the local bar, getting drunk and causing a commotion, minor vandalism, or attempting to expand the edges of their property right on to Warrior Peak Sanctuary land, it was enough that someone should step up and show them they weren't going to get away with it for another moment.

Xavier narrowed his eyes as he stared out on to the

dark road ahead of him. The main thing on his mind right now was Hannah. He had heard the fear in her voice when she said she wanted to go back inside the building, and he knew it wasn't just from the fall she'd taken.

It made him so angry to hear her like that—not angry at her, and not because she didn't have any reason to be afraid, but because he hadn't made this place safe enough for her to feel comfortable. She had been there on the night of the fire, and he could tell she still carried the psychological scars, just like he did. The dirty cops who had set fire to the lodge property months before had been dealt with, but everyone there was still dealing with the emotional fallout in their own ways. This incident had stirred all those feelings back up. So, it needed to be dealt with. Tonight.

"We're going to have to move everyone down to that crappy hotel in town if we can't get the heat back up and running by tomorrow morning," Lawson added. "This is a bad situation, Xavier. We need to make this quick. Everyone at the lodge will be feeling the cold soon. We need to find a fix fast."

"I know," Xavier muttered. The sanctuary grounds were supposed to be a safe place, a place where their guests could come to heal, where they could rely on Xavier and Lawson to provide them everything they needed. At this time of year, heat was the bare minimum. They would already be waking up to the freezing cold, and Xavier hated the thought of it.

All the more reason to go and confront the Haynes brothers and make sure they understood exactly how seriously Lawson and Xavier took the current situation. Even if they hadn't made the attack outright, they probably knew who did. Something told Xavier they had connections to every shady corner of this community. And Xavier had seen that there were far darker edges to this town than he would have liked to imagine.

They pulled the SUV up at the Haynes ranch. The small ranch house at the center of the property was lit up. Lawson and Xavier exchanged a look, and both of them climbed out of the vehicle. As they headed up to the building, the older brother, Dave, came stumbling out on to the porch. The air stank of booze and weed, the thick smell coming off the man in waves.

"What the hell are you doing here?" Dave called to them, clearly unable to tell who it was.

Xavier slowed his pace slightly. "We're here to talk," he replied. It was true, though he doubted that would be the only thing they did if they found out that either of the Haynes brothers had been involved in cutting off the power.

"It's too damn late for a social call," Dave protested, spitting off the porch just as Xavier reached the bottom step. He was stumbling drunk and had to grab on to the rickety porch railing to keep upright.

"Looks like you're still up," Lawson pointed out. "Just about."

Dave grinned, a crooked smile that didn't reach his eyes.

Xavier felt a wave of anger rush through him. These guys had been trouble for years, ever since he and Max were kids. Even back then, he hadn't liked either one of them, but if they were thinking of causing serious trouble at Warrior Peak, they had another think coming.

"Soooo what do you want to talk about at this time

of night?" Dave slurred, his eyes darting between the two men. They settled on Xavier for a moment, and he laughed and shook his head. "Haven't seen you around here since your little brother was throwing stink bombs on to my father's property," he sneered, still clearly holding a grudge against him for it. "What ever happened to Max anyway?"

Lawson sucked in a sharp breath, and Xavier took a step forward. Lawson grabbed his friend's arm to halt his progress.

Dave knew damn well what had happened to Max, and he was trying to get a rise out of Xavier by bringing him up. It was working. The animosity between them was heavy on the air but they didn't have time to get in a skirmish. They needed to ask their questions and be on their way. They still had the generators to worry about. Lawson let go of Xavier's arm and turned to Dave. "Look, we didn't come here for a fight. We just need to know if either of you were up at the lodge tonight?"

Confusion crossed Dave's face. "The lodge?" he asked, shaking his head. "What the hell would I want with that place?"

But before he could say another word, the door next to him opened, and Ron came out, holding a shotgun. It was aimed squarely at Xavier, though his grip was clearly shaky from all the partying they'd been doing.

"Get off our property," he snarled at Xavier, but Xavier wasn't going to take orders from someone like Ron. He grabbed the gun, twisting it out of Ron's hand with an almost comical ease. He checked the chamber—empty.

"Maybe try putting some bullets in next time, dumbass,"

Xavier told him, as he tossed the gun back to Ron. He caught it awkwardly, and Xavier took a step toward him.

"What about you?" he asked. "Were you up at the lodge tonight?"

"I don't know what the hell you're talking about." Ron was clearly delighted to frustrate Xavier.

"We've been here all night," Dave started waving his arm back and forth between himself and Ron. "Had a little party with some friends."

Xavier and Lawson shared a glance then Lawson stepped to the side to look through the open door. Sure enough, there were beer cans scattered around and what looked like a poker table set up inside. Lawson caught Xavier's eye and shook his head. It looked like they'd been set up here for a while playing cards. Plus, they looked too wasted to be behind a wheel. They could barely stand up without help.

"Any of your friends been there, that you know of? Or have you heard of anyone wanting to mess with us?" Xavier asked, watching them both for signs of nervousness or deceit.

Ron shook his head then walked toward the door, gesturing inside. "Look, man. Like my brother said, we've been here. We don't know anything about trouble. See for yourself." He motioned for the two men to step inside.

Xavier stepped forward and peeked inside, confirming what Lawson had seen. Poker table, chairs, snacks, and empty beer cans littered the area.

Lawson gestured to Xavier and turned toward the vehicle. Xavier followed his retreat, stopping at the bottom of the steps to leave the brothers with a warning.

"You guys stay away from the sanctuary property," Xavier told them both.

Ron rolled his eyes in exasperation. "Sure thing, captain!" He gave Xavier a mock salute. Dave snickered at his brother's antics.

Xavier shook his head in frustration as he settled behind the wheel.

"Make sure we don't see you there," Lawson warned them one more time, before climbing in the passenger seat.

Xavier felt the anger buzzing through his system, but now, it had nowhere to go. He doubted the brothers had anything to do with what had happened over at the lodge that night, given the state they were in. But even though they most likely didn't personally mess with the generators earlier didn't mean they were completely innocent.

They were known for causing all sorts of mischief, but it really didn't seem logical that they'd cause that kind of disruption in the middle of winter when they knew that the power was more important than ever at the lodge with guests inside.

"What do you think?" Lawson asked.

"I don't know," Xavier replied tersely.

It seemed unlikely the brothers would have managed to pull off something that focused and specific, even at the best of times. They weren't known for having a brain cell between them. Doing something like that would take actual coordination, and they didn't seem to have the capability to do that. They were more likely to use intimidation or petty destruction than they were to come to the sanctuary in freezing weather to cut the power. It seemed too specific, too direct.

Which meant someone else must have done it. But who? And did they have anything to do with the way Xavier's room had been rummaged through the other night? He doubted that had been the Haynes brothers. They would have been out of place and someone would have noticed. Whoever had done it clearly knew how to pull it off without leaving a trace of their identity. He was sure the clumsiness of the Haynes brothers would have left some sign of them behind.

"Me, neither," Lawson admitted with a sigh. "But we can keep an eye on them these next few days. They might not have done it themselves, but it seems like the kind of thing they might have paid or blackmailed someone to do."

"Could be," Xavier replied. He didn't bring up his room again—he was sure he didn't need to. Lawson would already have that on his mind right now, and Xavier didn't need to push it to the front of the conversation again.

"Anyway, we should get back to the lodge," Lawson added. "We're going to need the whole night to get the generators working again. And I don't want anyone to wake up tomorrow with no heat and nothing to eat."

Xavier could already feel his heart sinking at the prospect, but Lawson was right. As the guys who ran the place, they had a duty of care to everyone who stayed there, everyone who relied on them.

His mind drifted to Hannah before he could stop it. How quickly he reacted when he saw her hit the ground. It hadn't been intentional, but he knew Lawson would have noticed.

He had done everything he could to try to keep the truth of his feelings for her under wraps, but at times like this, they came out before he could stop them from showing. He just wanted her to be okay. The same thing had happened on the night of the fire. As soon as he had seen the flames licking the horizon, the first thing on his mind was what he could do to keep her safe.

He started the drive back to the sanctuary, lost in his thoughts, trying to nod in the right places as Lawson talked to him, discussing what they were going to do when they got back to the lodge.

Lawson frowned at him as Xavier pulled the SUV to a halt outside the lodge, looking over at him with an inquisitive expression again. "What's on your mind?" he asked.

Xavier tried to keep his face neutral. "Nothing. Just trying to figure out how we're going to fix the generators."

That was only half of the truth—and far removed from anything Lawson wouldn't have been able to take, especially with everything else they had to deal with right then. If Lawson had any idea Xavier was stuck thinking about his little sister, he would have freaked out.

It was safer for everyone if Xavier kept his mouth shut and focused on the task at hand. Even if the only thing on his mind right now was Hannah.

# Chapter Six

"I'm so sorry about last night," Hannah apologized again.

From the other side of the desk, Marnie grinned at her. "I was cozy in my bed," she replied. "I didn't even notice a thing, honestly. You've got nothing to be sorry for."

Hannah found that hard to believe. The power had been out almost all night before Xavier and Lawson managed to get it back on, and the lodge had been freezing. She was sure Marnie was just being polite so she could get on her way without making waves and start her new life.

It was hard to believe she'd already been there for three months; Hannah could still remember the day the middle-aged woman had arrived, fidgety and freaked out, a bruise over her left eye from the abusive ex she had just fled. Hannah had tried to calm her down that night, but she had been so terrified she was hardly able to take in a word Hannah said to her. But now? She looked like a whole different person. She was glowing, her bruises healed, and her face lit up with a bright, easy smile that came from a joy deep inside of her.

It hadn't been easy for her; Hannah knew that much. She had seen the work Marnie had done to keep on top of her scattered mental state and had seen her coming out of therapy appointments in tears more than once. But slowly, she had started to get her feet back under her again, settling in to her treatment plan at the sanctuary and making herself useful.

By the time February came around, she was already planning what she was going to do once she left, and she had organized a trip with her brother to move out to her new place across the state. A fresh start. With a restraining order in place against her ex, hopefully she would never have to worry about him again.

"I can't believe you're going," Hannah told her as she tucked away the keys to Marnie's room. It was a bittersweet moment, for sure. Of course, she was beyond happy that Marnie was able to get back on her feet and start over, but Hannah was going to miss her. It was always the same, when someone who had been there for a while moved on—difficult for Hannah not to let her emotions get the better of her.

"Oh me, neither," Marnie replied with a sigh. "I can still remember when I first got here. I never thought I would get to the point I am now. But…" She grinned, biting her lip. "Here we are."

"You've earned it," Hannah told her. "You put in so much hard work, Marnie. We're all so proud of you."

"Stop, you're going to make me cry," Marnie protested, fanning her hand in front of her face and laughing. "I don't want to look a mess when my brother gets here."

"Sorry, sorry," Hannah apologized, and she darted around the reception desk to give her a huge hug.

Marnie squeezed her back, as though she wasn't quite ready to let go yet. "Thank you, Hannah," she murmured to her. "For everything you've done."

Hannah didn't feel like she had done enough to earn

that kind of comment, but it still meant the world to her. Being able to make a difference like this, really help people in a practical way, it was everything she had always wanted. Working at Warrior Peak Sanctuary wasn't how she had expected to do it, but she was so happy with where she was and grateful for the opportunity to help people every day.

Hannah looked past Marnie to see a car pulling up outside the lodge doors in the parking lot. "Is that your brother?" she asked, nodding outside, and Marnie turned around.

"Yeah, that's him," she replied, quickly wiping away the tears that had slipped down her cheeks. "I should get going, I guess."

"You should," Hannah agreed, giving her hand a squeeze. "You keep in touch, okay? Let us know how things go at your new home."

"I will," Marnie replied, and she lingered for one more moment before she headed for the door. She embraced her brother as he climbed out of the car.

Hannah watched them happily before she made her way back behind the desk. She was just arranging a few intake papers for later in the month when a voice caught her attention.

"Uh, hello."

Her head snapped up, and she found herself staring at a man she had never seen before. She smiled quickly, trying to look as welcoming as possible. She was the first point of contact most people had with the sanctuary, and she wanted to make sure they felt safe from the moment they stepped through the door. "Hi," she greeted him. "Can I help you with anything?"

The man looked a little disheveled, with a beat-up backpack over one shoulder and scruffy stubble just shy of a beard that told Hannah it had been a while since he'd actually had a decent place to stay. He looked tired, with dark rings underneath his eyes, and his clothes were scuffed and smudged with various stains.

Racking her brain, she tried to remember if any new arrivals were scheduled to come in today. She couldn't remember anything, but maybe there had been a last-minute change of plans she hadn't been made aware of.

"Yeah," the man replied, rubbing the back of his neck worriedly.

Hannah looked him up and down; if ever there was a poster boy for ex-military, this guy would be it. He wore combat boots, an old army jacket and a pair of sweatpants that looked as though they had seen some action. The way he carried himself, too, told her that he had at least been through basic training. She ran into plenty of military guys working here, and she'd developed a sense for them.

"You here to visit someone?" she asked. Maybe he was just stopping by to catch up with an old friend.

He shook his head. "I came here because...because I want to check on your availability." He dropped his chin to his chest as he said it.

Hannah stared at him for a moment, surprised. It wasn't often they got walk-ins like this, but when they did, it was usually because the person was in need of some serious help. She quickly clicked through a program on her computer to see if there were any rooms free. She probably should have consulted with Xavier or her brother first, of course, but she knew they wouldn't want her turning away someone who was so clearly in need of help.

"We don't have any rooms in the lodge right now, but we try to keep a few cabins available for overflow guests. We have one you can use, if that's okay with you. It's only a short walk, and you'll still have access to everything here in the lodge," she said.

"No problem." She could hear the relief in his voice.

Where had this guy come from? Her mind was racing with questions, but she knew it wasn't her place to interrogate him just now. She wasn't even sure how he'd gotten up here. She hadn't seen a vehicle coming up the drive or heard one in the parking lot. She knew she would have noticed it, especially with Marnie's brother stopping by.

"Okay, sir, let me get a file started for you and then I'll go over a few other things with you." Hannah told the man, as she opened the computer program to log new arrivals.

"May I get your name and how long you'd like to stay?" She asked moving her hands to the keyboard.

The man hesitated and look around again before replying. "Jed. Jed Black. And I'm not sure yet, maybe a week or two."

"Nice to meet you, Mr. Black."

Hannah asked him a few basic questions, starting an intake file for him. She wasn't sure what to make of him, but he seemed fidgety and nervous, as though he was worried about something—or someone. But she was used to this, given the people she'd dealt with over the years. She knew better than to judge. He could have been through anything before he arrived here, and this might be his last resort. The last thing he needed was her judgment.

"Okay, so here's a key to cabin G3," she explained, pushing it over the counter toward him. "You can get settled and stay there tonight, and then you'll have a meeting with our resident psychiatrist, Dr. Sarah Peterson, at 9:00 a.m. tomorrow. She has an office just down that corridor, you can't miss it. Just take a left, and you'll see her name on the door. All our guests see her first for an assessment, then we'll make a treatment schedule for you to follow while you stay with us."

Jed paused for a moment, as though he wasn't sure he wanted to agree to the appointment.

"I know it seems intimidating," Hannah assured him. "But this is the best way we can evaluate your needs while you're staying with us. There's nothing to be worried about, she's a total professional, and she's not going to force you to talk about anything you don't want to in any great detail."

He breathed a sigh of relief. "Okay," he muttered, and he grabbed the key from the counter and tucked it into his pocket quickly. His eyes darted left and right, like he was waiting for someone to jump out at him at any moment. "I'll be there," he replied. "Wherever there is."

"I'll walk you to your cabin," Hannah offered. "And then I could come by first thing in the morning and walk you to Dr. Peterson's office, if you'd like."

"Sure. I really would," he agreed, and suddenly, he flashed her a smile.

She wasn't sure what it was about that smile, but it caught her off guard. He had been so reserved and so nervous up until now, and yet all of that seemed to fall away for a moment. Like it had just been an act he was putting on.

"Would you like to grab some coffee or a bite to eat

from the cafeteria before we head out to your cabin?" Hannah offered.

Jed shook his head. "No, thanks. I'd like to get settled in and cleaned up first, if you don't mind."

"Okay, let me grab my coat," she told him, and she made her way around the counter to get her jacket. It was still bitingly cold out there, and she could have sworn that the shower didn't feel as hot as it normally did when she had used in that morning. Might have just been her imagination, given that the generators had been out, but she was still chilly.

"I heard really good things about this place," Jed remarked.

She smiled and nodded. "Well deserved, trust me," she replied, zipping up her jacket and stuffing her hands into the pockets. "Do you need a hand with your bag?"

"I'm fine," he promised her. "Thanks for all your help, by the way. You're the best. Miss…?"

"Just call me Hannah," she replied.

"Hannah," he repeated, nodding. There was that smile again, broad, handsome, slightly disarming. She would bet he'd used that smile to get anything he wanted in the past, though clearly it hadn't worked out for him if he had wound up at the sanctuary.

"Well, let's get you settled. Shall we?" Hannah opened the door and motioned for Jed to precede her. He fell into step beside her as they walked down the path to his cabin.

## Chapter Seven

As the sound of chatter and plates clattering filled the communal dining hall, Xavier couldn't let himself relax. He knew this should be a chance for him to switch off after everything that had happened. After the stress of the generators going out last night, and then his encounter with the Haynes brothers and Dave mentioning Max, Xavier had ended up having nightmares when he finally made it to bed. He'd been up all night tossing and turning, trying to clear his mind so he could get a few hours of sleep.

He would much rather go to his room and eat there to avoid the noise and chaos, but he was sure his absence would be noted. He also didn't want to give whomever had sneaked into his room the heads-up that he was on to them.

Lawson was next to him, chatting away to Sarah, and Xavier knew his best friend would notice if he tried to slip away. He didn't want to deal with another interrogation about his well-being, but he was sure it was only a matter of time before Lawson brought up how Xavier should talk with Sarah to get passed the nightmares. He knew it was just Lawson trying to help, but the thought of dredging up his past like that seemed counterintuitive to him. He had always dealt with things on his own.

And this was no different.

Nor was the mission he was currently dedicated to—finding out who had broken into his room the other night while he had been down in the shower. He scanned the tables, trying to catch someone watching him. Something, anything he could draw from to figure out who it had been.

But everyone seemed caught up in their own conversation, not paying any attention to him.

Which was a good sign, really. Sarah had recently put forth the idea of bringing more of the guests into the day-to-day cooking and food preparation at the lodge. She thought it would be a good way to coax some of the more isolated members into a better, healthier headspace and more ordinary routine. So many of their guests had a habit of hiding out in their rooms and cutting themselves off from everyone else, but it wasn't going to do them any good in the long-term. Convincing them to help out with the cooking and cleaning might lead them to socialize more, giving them a sense of purpose that really helped with their recovery.

At least, that was what Sarah had said.

And, judging by the way everyone seemed to be chatting to each other right now, what she had suggested was making a difference. Xavier was always pleased to see people getting along, people coming out of their shell. He had struggled with socializing himself for a long time after he got back from overseas…and losing his brother. If he hadn't had the planning and setup of Warrior Peak

Sanctuary to focus on, he didn't know what he would have done.

All the more reason to be protective of what they'd built here. And precisely why he was smoking out the rat in their midst. Nobody seemed to be acting suspiciously, at least from what he could tell, and he usually had a pretty good eye for this stuff. His gaze was drawn to the far end of his table, where Hannah sat with a new arrival. Xavier hadn't had a chance to read his intake file yet, but it looked like he was settling in.

It was impossible not to feel at home around Hannah. Her beautiful honey-brown eyes sparkled when she smiled, and she had this way about her that was impossible to deny. A bright, bouncy energy that seemed to fill every room she stepped into.

Xavier glanced around the rest of the room, taking note of all the guests he'd interacted with and those who were new. Nothing seemed off with anyone. No odd looks, no one acting strange. His gaze tracked back to Hannah and the new guy. He had a strange feeling he'd seen him before. He'd have to think on it, maybe it would come to him later.

As though sensing his eyes on her, she glanced across the table at him, and he nodded in silent greeting. She flashed him a dazzling smile in return.

He tried to focus on the task at hand, sipping his water and keeping his eyes open for suspicious behavior. He didn't know what he was looking for, exactly, but he would know when he found it. He always did.

When everyone was finished, Hannah shooed the rest of them away. "Xavier and I will clean up," she announced.

Xavier rolled his eyes playfully. "Do I have to?" he asked like a whiny kid being forced to do chores.

Lawson laughed and slapped a hand on to his shoulder. "You can't keep getting away with doing nothing," he teased.

Xavier shook his head. "Wasn't fixing the generators last night enough?"

"Everyone has to pull their weight around here," Hannah told him cheerfully as she began gathering up the plates. "And you've got a lot of weight to pull. Come on, give me a hand. Let's start clearing the tables."

In truth, Xavier didn't mind at all having the opportunity to spend a little more time with Hannah alone. Even though he had sworn up and down to Lawson that nothing was going on between them, he still had feelings for her. How could he not? Her warm, bright kindness was impossibly attractive after he'd spent a lifetime working with people who shut that side of themselves off. And the way her freckles wrinkled when she smiled… Yeah, he still had it bad for her. He hoped it would pass eventually. It had to in order for him to maintain his friendship with Lawson.

The two of them started carting plates to the kitchen. As Xavier set about washing while Hannah dried, she glanced over at him. "What happened with the Haynes brothers last night?" she asked.

"Nothing," he admitted. "They were just drunk and talking crap like they always do. I don't think they actually had anything to do with the generators."

"You guys just took off last night," she remarked. "I had no idea what you were doing."

"Yeah, sorry," he apologized. He knew he owed her

more of an explanation. It wasn't just that they worked together, he had been friends with her for a long time, too. She had been there since day one of the sanctuary opening, and she'd always been a huge part of why people felt as safe and comfortable as they did here. If it hadn't been for her, it would have just been his grumpy ass at the reception desk, and he knew that wouldn't have been very welcoming for new arrivals.

"There's just been a lot on my mind," he admitted before he could stop himself. It was always like this with her—he could never stop himself from telling her the truth. He didn't want to worry her, but she was so easy to talk to that he couldn't help but share what was on his mind.

"Lodge stuff?" she asked. "Or...?" She lifted her finger to her temple and tapped the side of her head.

He shrugged. "Both, I guess," he replied quietly, handing her another plate.

Their fingers touched for the barest moment, and he had to draw his hand back quickly, hoping she hadn't felt the spark rushing between them. The two of them hadn't talked about their attraction or the kiss they shared since Lawson had blown up at them both about it, but he could tell it was still on her mind, too.

"You should talk to Sarah," she suggested.

"Yeah, that's what Lawson said, too."

She raised her eyebrows at him. "Well, you know how much I hate agreeing with my brother," she joked. "But maybe you should actually listen to him."

Xavier chuckled. "Yeah, maybe," he replied. "You know I'm not good at taking advice."

She smiled wryly. "Yeah, if you were, I might tell you

that you're doing a crappy job with these dishes," she teased, flipping one over in her hand demonstratively. "See? This one still has food on it."

"Hey, that's just an old stain," he protested, as he took the plate back from her.

She laughed. "Mmm, not sure I believe that. Here, why don't we swap? You probably can't screw up the drying part."

"I'm not screwing up the washing part, either," he replied, but he was laughing. Her attitude was infectious, even when he had so much on his mind. Sometimes, he felt like she was the only person who could force him out of his own head for a while and into the moment.

They scuffled for a moment over the dishes, and she dipped her hand into the water and pulled out a handful of fluffy suds, tossing them at him. "Here, soap," she teased. "It's that thing you're supposed to use to wash dishes, remember?"

"Oh, you mean this?" He grabbed a handful himself and launched it at her.

She shrieked and jumped out of the way, nearly knocking down a stack of plates piled up behind her on the counter. He reached past her to catch them.

She narrowed her eyes at him. "Oh, you are so going to pay for that," she warned him, and she grabbed some more suds, hurling them in his direction.

He dodged out of the way, ducking just in time, and the dishwater landed on the plates behind him. "You're going to clean those up," he shot back.

"Not a chance," she replied. "You were the one on washing duty, remember?"

But before she could say another word, Aaron appeared in the kitchen doorway and cleared his throat.

Both Hannah and Xavier spun around as soon as they heard him.

"You guys okay in here?" Aaron asked.

Xavier nodded, wiping off his hands. "Yeah, we're fine."

"Okay, good." Aaron cocked an eyebrow as he looked between them. "Because some of the guests are just settling down for the night, and they heard a ruckus and were worried that there was something going on down here."

Hannah and Xavier exchanged a glance, grinning like a pair of schoolkids who had been caught skipping classes.

"Sorry," Hannah apologized. "We'll keep it down."

"Thanks," Aaron replied, and he paused for another moment, looking between them. There was clearly some other comment he wanted to make, but he thought better of it, much to Xavier's relief. Last thing he needed was to have someone else speculating on what was going on between him and Hannah. It would drive Lawson insane if he found out that they were still flirting with each other, even after he had made it clear what he thought of that. Lawson had warned him off his sister because he didn't think Xavier was stable enough to be in a relationship and he didn't want Hannah to suffer because of it.

Aaron left, and Hannah pulled a face at Xavier.

"Guess we should get back to work," she told him. "Without scaring the guests."

"Guess so," Xavier agreed. "You want to wash this time?"

"I think I'll just supervise," she replied. "I don't trust

myself with those slippery plates, I can already see my-self breaking one."

"Okay, back to drying duty then," Xavier told her, nod-ding to the spot beside him.

She took her place and stole a glance at him out of the corner of her eye.

"What is it?" he asked her quietly. He wasn't sure what he wanted her to say, but he knew he had to find out what she was thinking.

She paused for a moment, biting her lip, like her mind was wandering to a million different places at once. "Nothing," she said finally, shaking her head. "I just… You know you can always talk to me, right? If some-thing's bothering you?"

"I know," he replied softly. He had no intention of bur-dening her with the information of the break-in; she didn't need to worry about him any more than she already did. But there was some relief in knowing that she was will-ing to listen to him. Sometimes, he felt like he was deal-ing with so much alone, so many of the memories in his mind still so fresh thanks to the nightmares he was being tortured with every night.

"Good," she replied, and she bumped her hip against his. The small touch alone was enough to make him smile, her closeness always welcome for him. "Back to work then, soldier."

They went back to washing and drying the dishes in companionable silence, but Xavier's mind was still wan-dering. Wandering back to all those nights he had woken up in his bed alone, and wondering if his nightmares might have eased up a little if he had been sleeping next to her instead.

# Chapter Eight

Hannah stared out the big window in the lodge's reception area, scanning the quiet grounds. She was so warm and comfy in the lodge, and she dreaded the thought of having to venture back out into the frosty morning.

She had come out early to help get breakfast made, and now she was going to walk Jed to his first meeting with Sarah so he'd know where her office was for future appointments. Letting out a big sigh, she wrapped her arms around herself in a futile attempt to ward off the cold, opened the door and made her way toward his cabin.

Shoving her hands deep in her pockets as she trudged down the misty path, she couldn't stop from wondering how much longer spring was going to take to show up.

Chatting with Jed last night, she had gotten a strange vibe from him. She couldn't quite put her finger on what it was, and she had dismissed it out of hand, convincing herself that it was nothing more than his trauma or stress making him act a little off. Once he got a little more settled here, she was sure she would feel more comfortable around him.

Reaching his cabin, she was just lifting her hand to knock on the door when it opened in front of her. She offered him a smile in greeting.

"Good morning," he announced, stepping out from the cabin quickly and closing it up tight behind him, like there was something in there he didn't want her to see.

"Hey," she greeted him. "You sleep okay?"

"Great, thanks," he replied, though the dark rings around his eyes told her differently.

She decided not to press the issue, and gestured back toward the lodge. "You ready for your meeting with Sarah?"

"Sure," he replied. "Lead on."

He kept pace with her as they made their way back to the main building. Something seemed to have shifted in him since the night before, and he was spilling his story to her before she had a chance to respond.

"I've heard so many good things about this place," he remarked brightly. "I wanted to come here for a long time. Got so much to work through, you know?"

She nodded, remembering him saying something similar the day before. "Lots of the guests here do," she replied. She wasn't going to delve any deeper, but there was something about the way he spoke that told her he wished she would.

"Yeah, wartime really does a number on you," he remarked. "I saw some pretty messed-up stuff out there."

He paused expectantly, but Hannah didn't take the bait. She didn't want to hear those stories. She knew he must have been through hell to end up here, but that didn't mean she had to go into the details first thing in the morning. "That's what Sarah's here for," she told him with a smile. "She's amazing at helping people work through their trauma. I bet you'll find her really helpful."

He paused as they stepped inside the lodge together

and rolled his shoulders back. A hint of defensiveness came off of him, and Hannah held his gaze steadily. She was better at managing grocery lists and intake forms than listening to people's deepest, darkest secrets, and she wanted to keep it that way.

But the way he was looking at her, it was clear he felt she'd said the wrong thing. Did he expect her to sympathize, tell him how sorry she was? Maybe she had been too blunt. Just as she parted her lips to apologize, footsteps caught her attention, and she turned to see Xavier approaching the two of them.

"Oh, Xavier," she greeted him, glad for the distraction. "This is Jed, one of our new arrivals."

Xavier extended his hand to Jed, and it seemed as though his presence instantly shifted something in Jed's mood. Jed cast aside the grim expression on his face and put on a smile instead, shaking Xavier's hand enthusiastically.

"Good to meet you," he remarked jovially. "You're one of the owners, right?"

"Yeah, I am," Xavier replied.

Hannah's ears perked up. Wait, how did Jed know that? He must have really been doing his research on Warrior Peak before he got here.

"Well, I think I can take it from here," Jed told Hannah. "You said the therapy office was down there, right?" He pointed down the corridor.

Hannah nodded.

"Thanks for your help," he told her, and then he took off down the hallway.

Hannah watched him as he went, and so did Xavier. Xavier had always had a good eye for people, and she was sure he could tell as much as she could that something was off here. "What's up with him?" she wondered quietly.

"I don't know," he admitted. "But he reminds me of someone."

Hannah looked to him in surprise. "Reminds you of someone? Who?"

"Not sure, there's just something familiar feeling." Xavier shrugged and turned his attention to Hannah. "I need to head into town to see Sheriff Willis, want to come along?"

She felt a smile spread over her face before she could stop it. Time alone with him? Yes, please. "Sure," she agreed.

They headed out to his SUV, where Hannah cranked up the heat. She was still freezing from her trek to get Jed earlier, and the way his tone had shifted when Xavier walked up had sent a shiver down her spine in a way she couldn't quite understand.

"So what do you need to see the sheriff about?" she asked.

Xavier paused before he responded, his eyes fixed on the road in front of him, as though he was considering exactly what he was going to tell her.

*God, he looks so handsome in this light, the way it picks up the sharpness of his jawline...*

"There was a break-in at the lodge earlier this week," he explained. "One of the rooms. Mine, to be precise."

"Oh no way," she gasped, panic gripping her chest. "Did they take anything?"

"Can't seem to find anything missing," he replied, shaking his head. "So probably not, but I wanted to check in with Sheriff Willis anyway. Especially after the generators were taken out the other night."

"You think there's a connection?" she wondered aloud.

"Could be," he replied. "Better to be safe than sorry."

"Does anything ever go smoothly at Warrior Peak?" she remarked, only mostly joking.

Xavier turned one of the heating vents toward her, apparently noticing she still felt chilled. "It will," he assured her.

She couldn't help but notice how tense he was right now, the way the tendons in his arm flexed when he palmed the wheel. He was clearly anxious, and she wondered how much was going on that she had no idea about. She got it, she really did. Hannah wasn't involved in the big decisions of the day-to-day running of the sanctuary, and she didn't need to know every little detail. After the fire, though, she felt as if she should have been kept a little more in the loop with whatever went on around the place. She did live there, too, after all.

But she knew it went deeper than that for Xavier. Of course it did. She knew what he had lost when he was in the army. His little brother had followed him into active service and had died out there—right in front of Xavier, from what Lawson had told her. She couldn't even imagine what that must have been like.

And that would have been bad enough, but when he came home, his parents blamed him for the loss. The funeral had been a mess—his mother jumping on the coffin while Xavier tried to hold her back, only for her to turn around and blame him publicly for Max's death. Hannah hadn't been there, but she'd heard about that from Lawson, too, and it made her chest ache to think of what that must have done to him.

Xavier had been grieving, too. She didn't know why his family had a hard time seeing that. She understood that it was normal for grieving people to look for someone to blame, but he had needed their support instead of their guilt and accusations. He was the one who had to watch Max die, after all.

The family went to pieces after that.

His parents passed away one after another—first his father, then his mother. She was hardly speaking to Xavier, even when she was on her deathbed, and Xavier had been left alone to bear the brunt of everything that had happened, all the pain and suffering that his family had struggled through.

Hannah had no idea how he even kept his head up sometimes. She couldn't imagine carrying on in the face of losing so many people close to her, let alone knowing that most of them blamed her for kicking off the chain of events that led them down that path. All of it just felt utterly sick and twisted, but here he was, still standing.

Even if sometimes it looked as though he wanted to fall apart entirely.

But he didn't. He held himself together, and Hannah knew a big part of that was because he felt so much responsibility to the people at Warrior Peak Sanctuary. He had worked hard to make it as safe a space as he could for those who were going through so much of the same trauma as he had.

If it hadn't been for his dedication, she was certain there were those who wouldn't have made it through at all. The struggle they faced was so unique, sometimes they needed people around them who really got it, rather than some expert who only had a distant understanding of what it must have been like.

But Hannah wondered why he couldn't extend the same kindness to himself. He must have needed the support, especially after what he had been through, but he always seemed to reject it. Maybe he didn't feel as though he was worthy of it, given the way his parents had turned on him when he lost his brother. It wouldn't have surprised her.

He must have taken some of their blame to heart, even if it was wildly misplaced. She had heard a little about his brother from Lawson, and she knew that Xavier would have done anything to look out for him. Like he did now for the guests of Warrior Peak.

As they wound their way down the mountain into Blue Ridge, Hannah watched Xavier out of the corner of her eye. She had tried to talk to him about getting help before, when they were doing the dishes, but he seemed to just brush her off without really taking any of their conversation to heart.

And she understood that. It had to be painful to bring all those memories back to the surface again. But he couldn't keep living like this—torturing himself, treating himself like the perpetrator when she was sure he did everything he could to protect Max. Hannah knew Xavier would have given his own life in Max's place if he could have.

Though, if what he was saying about the break-in was true, she understood why he felt like he had more important things than his mental health to focus on. There could be someone targeting the lodge again.

The thought of that happening, their safe space being violated again, spooked the hell out of her. She knew it worried Xavier and Lawson, too.

She focused her gaze on the road ahead of her as they pulled into town and Xavier took a turn to head to the police station. She silently promised herself she was going to do everything she could to help keep the sanctuary—and the people who relied on it—safe.

# Chapter Nine

"Be sure to reach out if there's any other disturbance," Sheriff Willis told Xavier as he walked him to the door of the police station.

Xavier nodded. "Anyone looks at me funny, you'll be the first to hear about it," he assured him.

Willis nodded and reached out his hand to shake Xavier's. "Thanks for coming in," he told him. "We'll file those reports today, make sure there's a paper trail if anything else happens."

Xavier shook his hand in appreciation. Having the local cops on their side, at least, was something. Willis was a good guy, and they'd had a positive relationship with the local police with him as sheriff. Warrior Peak had done a lot of work with former police as well as former military, and Willis appreciated the work they did to get them back on their feet.

"You think it's going to help?" Hannah asked Xavier as they stepped back out on to the street.

"I don't know," Xavier admitted. "But at least we have a case open if something else does happen."

"Yeah, I guess that has to count for something," she agreed, but she sounded pretty doubtful.

Xavier felt a twinge of guilt for telling her about the

break-in, but he knew there would be no point in hiding it from her. She could always guess when something was going on inside his head, and he was done pretending otherwise.

He felt a little better now that he had told Willis about what happened. Xavier had filled him in on everything, from the break-in in his room to the generators going out and their trip to the Haynes' brothers' ranch—though Xavier had added that he and Lawson were pretty sure the brothers had nothing to do with what had gone down.

"You want to get something to eat while we're here?" Xavier suggested. He knew he and Hannah should probably be getting back to the lodge, but it wasn't often he got to spend time alone with her, and he didn't want to waste it. Yes, he knew he shouldn't be doing anything to encourage his feelings for her, but they were friends, right? And friends sometimes got lunch together. It didn't have to mean anything.

"That sounds great," she agreed. "I'm starving. I hardly got breakfast this morning before I had to go meet Jed."

Jed. There was another nudge at the back of Xavier's mind, though he was sure he had no reason to be suspicious of the new arrival. He had only just gotten to Warrior Peak, so the chance of him being involved with everything that had been going on was next to zero.

They drove to the closest café down the street. Mary Cinder, who owned the fabric store next door, was just gathering herself from the last table by the window to go back to work.

"Oh, you two take this table," she told them. "I should be getting back to the store anyway."

"Thanks, Mary," Hannah replied with a smile, taking a seat at the vacated table.

Xavier ordered for the two of them at the counter before he came back to join her. He knew what she liked—he always paid attention to what she chose at mealtimes, taking in all those little details about her that he doubted she even paid much mind to herself.

Returning to the table, he noticed a line of lingering frost around the edge of the window. Hannah had noticed it, too, and she sighed.

"I can't wait for spring," she remarked to him. "Winter lasts way too long here. I do enjoy my cool morning walks, but I feel like I'm going to freeze to death before I see the flowers bloom."

"Yeah, agreed," he replied.

Back when he had been growing up, winter had been his favorite time of the year. He had counted down the days until the first snow, when he and Max could go out and have a snowball fight and sled down the large hill behind their house. Their hands would burn with the frozen cold when they came in, and their mom would always have a hot cocoa ready and waiting for them on the stove when they got back. He could still remember that sweet aroma, the way it smelled like home to him.

He suddenly realized Hannah was staring at him, a small smile on her face, while he'd been lost in his head. "What is it?" he asked, shifting slightly in his seat.

"Nothing," she replied, shaking her head. "You just looked…content there for a moment. I don't see that a lot in you."

He grimaced. Yeah, she had a point there. Especially these last few months, as much as he had tried to pretend otherwise. He had been on edge, tormented by the memories of losing his brother, and he knew he hadn't been doing a good job of hiding it.

"Winters have always been long here," he remarked, changing the subject. "Ever since I was a kid. My brother and I—" The words were out before he could stop them, but he clammed up the moment they were out of his mouth.

Hannah must have been able to tell how much his memories got to him. "I like hearing about the sanctuary when it was your family home," she told him, offering him a smile. "And about your brother. Max, right?"

Hearing her say his name like that made him tense. He flinched, and she must have noticed. She reached across the table and placed her hand on top of his. Her touch took him back to a better place—a place where he had never lost his brother, where the pain of what he had been through didn't weigh so heavily on him. Warm, full of love and light, where he didn't carry the shame of what he had done.

Or what he had failed to do.

"Yeah, Max," he replied, reaching his thumb up to brush against her skin. This was dangerous, too dangerous. He should have stopped it before it went any further, but how the hell could he, when having her this close felt so right? He felt the electricity racing from her skin to his.

"You should talk to Sarah," she suggested again, and he drew his hand back at once. He could feel that defensiveness rising inside of him, that urge to push back against what she was suggesting and tell her to back off. "I don't want to go through all that again," he muttered.

"You don't have to talk about the bad stuff right away,"

she suggested. "You could start with the good memories. The stuff you want to remember."

He drew his gaze away from her and shook his head. "It's not a good idea."

"I'm worried about you, Xavier," she told him, a sadness to her voice. "I know... I can see how much you've been struggling. I just want the best for you."

He didn't know what to say. Thankfully, he didn't have to come up with anything, because the cheery waitress arrived with their food a moment later, placing it in front of them as she chattered away about the weather.

Hannah sighed, clearly seeing that the moment was lost, and tucked in to her meal.

Afterward, when they stepped outside, she seemed subdued. Xavier could tell she was still bothered by the conversation they'd had before lunch. It would have been easy for him to just leave it there and hope she didn't bring it up again, but something in him was urging him to tell her more. No matter how much it hurt, no matter how much it dredged up for him. She was trying to reach out, trying to make a difference, and she deserved more than to just be brushed off.

He didn't look at her as he spoke. "I'm sorry for shutting you out."

She glanced up at him in surprise. "What do you mean?"

He still didn't meet her gaze. "I know you're trying to help," he explained. "With the...the stuff with Sarah, I mean. But I just can't go back there and pull all those memories up again. They're bad enough as it is, with the dreams and everything..."

"The dreams?" she asked softly.

"I—I used to have these dreams all the time, about what happened to my brother," he continued, stilted. He wasn't used to being this honest with anyone, let alone her, and making himself so vulnerable felt like a mistake. He had held it all in for so long, so how could telling the truth fix any of this? "And I thought they were done a long time ago," he went on. "Actually, they were. Up until the night of the fire. Ever since then, I've been…dealing with them again. I don't think I've made it through a whole night without having them at some point."

"But the fire was nearly three months ago," she whispered.

He grimaced. "Yeah. I know."

She fell silent for a moment and followed behind him as they made their way back to his vehicle. It was obvious she still had a lot of questions, but he wasn't sure he had it in him to keep answering. Even sharing that much hurt. It brought to mind all the memories of Max that Xavier had been torturing himself with for so long now.

He wished he could just focus on the good times, but every time his beloved baby brother came into his mind, it was with the harsh reminder of how he had been lost. How Xavier had been there, right there next to him, and unable to stop it. Maybe his mom had been right when she blamed him for his brother's death.

How could he have let it happen?

Whenever he closed his eyes, that was all he could see. Fire, blood, the sudden blank look in Max's eyes, the blooming red stain on his neck running down his camouflage uniform as he fell to the ground. Nothing could have saved him, but that didn't mean that Xavier didn't wish he had tried. He had been so frozen in shock and horror, he had taken vital seconds to snap back into reality, and if he had acted sooner...

He climbed into the SUV, and Hannah scrambled in the other side, not taking her eyes off of him. Gripping the wheel, he kept staring straight ahead. Had he said too much? Maybe now she thought he was weak, pathetic for being so consumed by the memory of what had happened.

But if she wanted to know, he would do his best to be open with her. She was about the only person in his life he felt like he could be honest with about this, even if he didn't know why.

No, that wasn't true. He knew exactly why. As much as he might have tried to deny it, it was the same reason he had been so shaken after the fire. He had seen far worse, far more violence than that, but it was the first time in a long time that he felt like he had a life worth protecting.

Like he had someone in his life he wanted to protect.

Instead of sitting in the passenger seat like he expected, Hannah got to her knees on the seat, not taking her eyes off of him. He turned to her, confused, and before he could say anything, she launched herself into his arms, wrapping herself around him, one hand at the back of his neck and the other slowly rubbing against his shoulder.

He thought about pushing her away, setting her back in her own seat, he really did. Maybe a stronger man would have, but he knew that he couldn't. It felt too good to have her that close. As soon as she touched him, he felt everything else just fall away, all the fight he'd had to keep his distance vanishing.

"It's going to be okay, Xavier," she murmured to him.

He couldn't think of anything to say back, but he didn't need to. Instead, he slipped his arms around her waist and pulled her in even closer to him. The scent of her shampoo and perfume filled the air around him, creating this little protective bubble that seemed to keep them safe from the rest of the world. He didn't care what anyone else thought in that moment. The only thing that mattered to him was the feel of her small, strong body pressed against his and her promise that everything was going to be okay.

Because, when she said it, he could almost believe her.

## Chapter Ten

The embrace caught her off guard, but it felt so deliciously good, Hannah couldn't find it in herself to pull back. The pressure of his strong hands around her waist, pulling her in close; the feel of his breath on her neck… All those touches that she had craved for so long but denied herself for fear that it would just drive a deeper wedge between her and her brother.

But now, here, in the quiet of the vehicle, there was no way either of them could deny it, this sweetness between them, this need. She pressed her head into his shoulder, inhaling the scent of him, and wondering how she had lasted so long without this.

When she pulled back slightly and looked into his eyes, she had no idea how he would react. Would he push her off, tell her they couldn't do this? Or would he give her what she had needed for so long?

Her heart slammed up against her ribs as he slowly lifted his hand to her face and cupped her cheek. His thumb rubbed against her skin in slow, soft motions.

And then, at last, he dipped in close and kissed her.

It wasn't a peck—it was a real kiss, a kiss that tingled from the top of her scalp to the very bottom of her toes. She smiled against his mouth and pressed herself into him, arching her back so she could show him just how much she wanted him. Nothing else made sense to her right now but the feeling of his mouth against hers, his tongue caressing the inside of her lip, a soft, delicious tease that made her whole body light up.

When he drew away from the kiss, he was breathing hard, but there was a smile on his face. She gazed at him, a little more nervous than she would care to admit. But God, that smile—it was everything to her. When she saw him smile, she knew there was no denying it. She was in love with him. She had been for years now, for so long she had lost track of it, but that didn't matter.

The way he kissed her, she knew he loved her, too.

"We should get back to the sanctuary," she murmured reluctantly. "Someone'll notice we're both gone."

"Yeah, someone like your brother." He sighed.

She pulled a face. "Oh don't bring him up. Let me pretend we can get away with this a little longer, huh?"

He chuckled and lifted his hand to her cheek again, gazing at her as though he could hardly believe she was right there in front of him.

She tilted her face into his palm, enjoying the feel of his calloused hands against her skin. She wasn't sure she would ever get tired of it—there was something addictive about the way he touched her, even when her good sense told her she should be holding back.

She leaned in and kissed him softly once more before pulling away and resituating herself on her own side of the SUV. She immediately missed his warmth.

"You think he's going to be angry again if he finds out?" Xavier asked as he took the wheel once more.

She shrugged. "Maybe," she admitted. "But we've done

a lot of talking since that first kiss all those months ago, you know. By now, Lawson's got to see that he was acting like an idiot. Big brother or not, he has no right to tell me, or you, how to live our lives. If we like each other..." She trailed off.

*Like* was far too weak of a word for everything she felt for Xavier right now, but she didn't want to jinx what had just happened by overstating it.

"He'll just have to get used to it," he finished up for her.

"My thoughts exactly. But we should still get back to the sanctuary—catch everyone up on what happened with the sheriff."

"Agreed," he replied, and he turned the key in the ignition and pulled away from the café.

She couldn't stop staring at him, now that she knew he felt at least some of what she did for him. For so long, she had denied herself this—this closeness, these sweet moments where they could just be together. She hoped this would be the start of him opening himself up a little, too. Maybe to her, maybe to Sarah; it didn't matter as long as he got some of the weight off his mind.

As they drove, heading up the mountain road that led through the dense forest and back to Warrior Peak, he glanced out the window at the passing scenery.

"Remind you of growing up here?" she asked.

He nodded. "Yeah, my brother and I used to play in these woods a lot when we were young," he remarked, smiling slightly. "I think it drove my mom insane. Max was always getting into trouble, falling out of trees, stuff like that. I can't count the number of times I would get yelled at when we came home and he had another scrape on his elbow."

"So he was kind of a daredevil then?" she prompted. She liked hearing these stories about his youth. It felt as though she was seeing some hidden side of him, something he did his best to keep from everyone else. It might do him good to reflect on some of the happier memories he had of his childhood. No matter how dark things had gotten, it didn't mean he had to leave behind everything good that had ever happened.

"I think he liked everyone to think he was," he replied, amused. "But you should have seen him when he was younger. He would come to my room at least twice a week, asking me to check under his bed for monsters. Or to sleep on the floor to keep him safe."

"And did you?"

"Of course I did." He laughed. "I couldn't turn him down, and he knew it. Anything he wanted from me, he got."

"Damn, I didn't realize you could have that kind of power over your big brother," she joked. "I should have tried to get more out of Lawson growing up."

"He didn't do all of that for you?"

"He did some of it," she replied. "But grudgingly. Don't know why he's got such a stick up his butt about protecting me now."

"Maybe because he's seen a bit more of the world," Xavier suggested. "He knows what can be out there if you're not careful. He just doesn't want you to have to deal with any of that."

"Yeah, I guess," she agreed.

She tried not to get upset with her brother, knowing that he was just looking out for her. But she didn't understand how he could feel like her being with Xavier was anything other than a good thing. If there was anyone in the world he trusted, it should be his best friend, right?

Well, they would figure that out when it came up again. For now, what mattered was the relaxed smile on Xavier's face as they drove. He reached out to give her leg a squeeze, his touch casual and easy, just as she had always wanted it to be.

"I love spending this time with you," she blurted out before she could stop herself. "I know I tried to keep my distance after what happened with my brother, but…" She trailed off with a shrug.

"Me, too," Xavier assured her, grinning.

She wished she could take a snapshot of his face like that and commit it to memory. She never wanted to forget the way he looked at her, the way it made her feel like she could take on the world and win.

"So you guys played a lot out here in the winter, too?" she asked, turning her attention back to the forest outside. "You must have been freezing."

"Yeah, but we always had a warm home to go back to," he replied. "We never wandered too far. Mom was always waiting, ready with a hot drink and a bandage for any bruises Max got along the way."

"Oh don't act like you didn't get a few, too," she teased.

He chuckled. "Yeah, okay, maybe I did sometimes, too," he admitted. "I wasn't always the sensible older brother."

She could hardly imagine him like that, relaxed and fooling around. All the time she had known him, he had seemed to be this solid, strong guy who took everything seriously—well, everything outside of her, of course. She always tried to bring out a lighter side of him, never wanting him to feel like he had to put up that front when he was with her. She wanted to see the man underneath, the man who had grown up from that little boy who had played in the snow with his baby brother.

"But in my defense, I..." Xavier began, but then, he sharply cut himself off, his words faltering as he looked in the rearview mirror.

Hannah craned her head around to see what he was looking at, and her stomach lurched. A big truck was racing up on them from behind.

The two-lane road was winding with a ravine on one side and a fast-flowing river on the other; the entire length of it was a no-pass zone. If another driver happened to be coming down the mountain, it would be bad for them all. As the truck sped toward them faster than anyone needed to on an icy road, she couldn't help but feel a familiar terror curling inside her stomach.

"Who the hell is that?" he muttered. "And why are they coming at us so fast? It's icy as hell out there."

"Maybe they're just trying to pass?" she offered optimistically, but she knew that wasn't the case. Nobody would dare speed around these mountain roads in this weather unless they were stupid. Or trying to intimidate someone.

Or drive them off the road.

"No, that's not it," he replied, his voice dropping to a growl. "You're buckled in, right?"

"Yeah," she squeaked, hoping he couldn't hear the fear in her voice. She could hear the other vehicle's engine on the road now, drawing ever closer, and it took everything she had not to let the panic get the better of her. Her eyes slid to the sides of the road—noting how close their SUV was to the edge. She shivered at the thought of how frigid that water must be.

"It's okay," Xavier murmured to her, sensing her tension.

She clasped her trembling hands in her lap. She wanted to believe him, God, she wanted to believe him, but she was struggling to contain her panic. After the fire, she hadn't been able to assume anything was innocent. Any danger in her vicinity, she was hyperaware of it.

Then the big truck was beside them on a curve. With the vehicles almost pressed up against each other, Hannah tried to look around Xavier to see the driver of the truck, but in her panicked state, she couldn't get a good look through the darkened windows.

Suddenly, the driver twisted the wheel and slammed their truck into Xavier's SUV.

"Hold on!" Xavier yelled, but his voice sounded far away.

Hannah's head spun, and everything slowed as the vehicle flipped off the road. The sickening crunch of metal and the sound of tearing filled the air, and she felt her scream stick in her throat. She wanted to yell out for help, but she knew it was no use.

But as their SUV spun through the air and down toward the water below, she finally let it out. A scream that bounced around the interior of the vehicle, her hands scrambling for purchase on something, anything.

But it wasn't enough to brace for the final impact as the SUV landed with a crash in the cold, murky river.

# *Chapter Eleven*

Xavier sucked in a long breath, trying to ground himself as the SUV finally came to a halt in the river several feet from shore. It was upside-down in the water, the sunroof smashed, and the freezing, dark liquid was starting to inch in through the gap between the doors and the roof.

"Xavier…" Hannah whimpered, and he reached over to squeeze her hand.

"It's going to be okay," he told her, as calmly as he could. "Just unbuckle your belt. We can get out of here."

She reached down to hit the button to release her seat belt, but it didn't budge. She stabbed at it a few more times, growing increasingly desperate, and then turned to him, eyes wide. "It's stuck," she told him.

Xavier grimaced and reached for the glove box where he kept a small blade. It would be enough to free her if he could get to it. But he couldn't reach the compartment from his side, restricted by his own belt. In order to help Hannah, he had no choice but to unclip it and let himself fall into the rapidly rising water below.

"Just hold on, I'm going to get you out," he promised her, and he unclipped his belt. Thankfully his wasn't stuck, and he landed with a grunt on the roof of the SUV.

No matter what it took, he was going to get them both out before the vehicle completely filled with water.

The ends of Hannah's dark brown hair were already dangling into the freezing water, making them look more black than brown. In a few minutes, it would reach her face as the SUV continued to slide deeper into the river as more water rushed inside.

He grabbed the door handle and heaved himself up toward the dashboard, pressing the button to release the small compartment where he kept his knife. It didn't budge. Damn. Was anything still working in this thing?

"What are you doing?" Hannah asked. He could hear the terror in her voice, and he wished he could stop to comfort her, but he knew he needed to keep focused on the task at hand before it was too late.

"I'm getting a knife to cut you free," he told her through chattering teeth. He could feel the chill of the water starting to set into his bones, and he knew they wouldn't last long out here without some help—but he could deal with that when the time came. What mattered now was getting that blade, cutting Hannah out of her seat belt and getting them out of this vehicle before it filled up or moved farther into the river.

He slammed his fist into the glove box a couple of times, until he felt the spring lock break, and it fell open. A bunch of stuff dumped out—maps, pens, a notepad, a granola bar—and he managed to catch the small knife before it dropped into the water below. Wrapping his hand around the handle, he turned to Hannah. "Can you pull the belt taut?"

The water was inching higher now, reaching her hairline, but she nodded, shivering. Taking the belt in her hand, she pulled it hard to create an easy surface for him to cut into.

"P-p-lea-se hurry," she begged him through her own chattering teeth, as though he would have done anything else.

He brought the blade to the thick fabric of the belt and started to saw at it, all too aware of how quickly the water was inching up her face. "It's going to be okay."

She let out another whimper as the water reached her eyes. She squeezed them shut, and her grip tightened on the belt. The fabric was starting to fray now, and he knew it was only going to be a few more seconds until it—

It snapped. Xavier dropped the blade and reached out to catch her before she fell into the roof of the vehicle, pulling her into his arms.

She gasped, wiping the water from her eyes, clinging on to him for dear life.

"You okay?" he asked her, and she managed to nod, though he could tell she was having a hard time pulling herself together. She gripped him tightly.

"We need to get out of here," she told him, voice shaking. "Are the doors stuck?"

He tried the handle on her side, but it wouldn't move. The SUV had sunk too far, and the water pressure on the doors was too great.

"Looks like it," he replied. "Here, go over toward the driver side—get back as far as you can."

He set her down next to the driver seat, and she wrapped her arms around the back of it for purchase as he pulled back to slam his foot into the opposite door. It didn't budge, but he could hear the metal groaning underneath the pressure. Going again, he mustered up all the force he had in him—not that there was much of it left. He was running on pure adrenaline now, doing his best to ignore the shock of the accident and the cold water. But it was just a matter of time before his body shut down.

He kicked again, and again.

Thankfully, on the fourth kick, the door finally came loose, leaving a gap large enough for him to get his hands in between the door and the frame.

Unfortunately, the opening also gave enough room for the frigid river to come rushing in as well. The SUV started filling faster, the water no longer held at bay. Reaching back for Hannah's hand, Xavier continued to push against the force of the icy river, using his shoulder and dragging Hannah out behind him.

The water they were in was only about chest deep for him, a little more for Hannah, but they struggled to trudge back to dry land through the freezing, mucky water.

"Thank God," Hannah breathed as soon as they were out of the water. They collapsed on the riverbank, and Xavier shot a look up to the road to make sure the person who had done this to them wasn't still there.

But it was totally quiet.

Whoever had taken them out had made a run for it already. A good thing, because even though Xavier was exhausted and fighting off hypothermia, he thought he probably could have mustered the strength to kill them with his bare hands for almost ending Hannah's life.

Did they think they had finished her and Xavier off? Or was this just meant to be a warning, a sign for them to keep their heads down and out of whatever trouble these people didn't want them knowing about?

He didn't know, but he was definitely going to get to the bottom of it.

Xavier wrapped a protective arm around Hannah, squeezing her in close. He could feel her shivering from the icy water as well as the cooler temperature, and he wished there was something he could do to make it better. He was wearing a jacket, but it wouldn't provide her any warmth because it was soaking wet. Their best bet was to get back to Warrior Peak Sanctuary as soon as possible and into dry clothes.

"How f-f-far are we from the lodge?" Hannah asked, and he looked over at her. There was a bloody mark on her head, just below her hairline.

"You're bleeding," he murmured.

She reached up to touch her head and pulled her hand away with a smear of blood on her fingers. Her eyes widened.

"Do you feel dizzy?" Xavier asked. "Nauseous?"

She shook her head. "N-no, nothing l-l-like that," she stuttered, but she winced. "I do have a bit of a headache, though."

"Okay, we need to get you checked out," he replied, and he steered her up toward the road. "Once we get back to the lodge, we'll get you looked over."

"And how a-are we going to g-get back there?" she asked, her voice laced with panic. "I mean, it's too far to walk, and it's too cold this time of the year, plus we're soaking wet, and we'll probably freeze to death…"

"I'll flag down a car," he replied before she spiraled any further. He was doing his best to keep her calm, though he could tell that she was on the brink of losing it completely. He smoothed a hand over her back, trying to soothe her. "You stay here," he told her. "I'll find some-one. I promise."

She parted her lips to protest, but the fight seemed to leave her just as soon as she had thought of it.

He knew as well as she did that there weren't many cars that came around this way at this time of year, and they would have to get seriously lucky to run into one. But he had to believe they would. The thought of being trapped out here, in the cold, with her bleeding head wound... No, he couldn't even consider it. He had to get them out of there as quickly as possible.

He could feel the chill start to settle in his bones and slow down his movements, but he tried to ignore it. He had dealt with worse.

He looked up and down the road, trying to make out any oncoming headlights that might indicate someone coming to help them, but there was nothing. What if the people who had driven them off the road came back to finish the job? He would fight with everything he had if he needed to, but he wasn't sure how much of a chance he stood against them, especially if they were armed.

Silence filled the air around him, and fear started to tug at the corners of his mind. He couldn't let anything happen to Hannah. He had lost too much already, and he wasn't going to lose her. He would do anything in his power to protect her.

Glancing back down the bank to check on her, he could see her eyes starting to droop as the shock and adrenaline wore off. He was about to run down to keep her awake when the sound of an engine drew his attention.

He spun around to see a car coming up the road to-ward them. He stepped out on to the pavement, lifting his hands above his head to flag it down. There was no way the driver would be able to ignore him, standing right in the middle of the road.

The car screeched to a halt in front of him, sliding slightly on the icy road. When an older man stepped out, Xavier lifted his hand to shield his eyes from the glare of the headlights and recognized Mr. Barkley, one of the local farmers he occasionally saw at a bar in Blue Ridge when he went to grab a drink. Mr. Barkley s walked to the front of the car, and stopped a few feet in front of Xavier and frowned when he realized who was standing in the road.

"Thank God," Xavier breathed. "We need your help. I'll be right back."

"Xavier?" the farmer asked his retreating form. "What are you…?"

But Xavier rushed down the bank, pulled Hannah into his arms and carried her up to the car. She might have been able to walk, but he didn't want her wasting any more of her energy.

"We need a lift," he told Mr. Barkley quickly. "Do you have any blankets in there? She's frozen."

The man nodded, and he pulled a couple of scratchy woolen blankets from the trunk of the car while Xavier helped Hannah into the back seat. Xavier shook the second blanket out before sliding in behind her, then pulled her close and wrapped it around them both.

Hannah's grip on him was firm, as though she didn't want to let go, and he shifted more into the seat to pull her tighter against him.

"What happened?" Mr. Barkley asked, clearly confused as he climbed into the driver seat once more.

Xavier guided Hannah's head to rest on his shoulder, not caring about her damp hair. He just wanted her close, where he could keep an eye on her. "We had an accident," he lied swiftly. He had no reason to think the farmer was in on anything, but there wasn't a chance in hell he was going to risk it.

"You want me to take you to the police station?" Mr. Barkley asked, putting the car in Drive.

Xavier shook his head. "Up to Warrior Peak Sanctuary, please," he told him, and the old man started driving up the mountain.

Xavier carefully stroked Hannah's hair and checked her wound again. It didn't look too bad from where he was sitting, but it was still bleeding some. He wanted to get her back and looked at by a medical professional. If anything had happened to her, if she had really gotten hurt while she had been with him...

He would never forgive himself.

More to the point, he would never forgive the people who had done this to her.

He was going to make them pay in any way he could.

# Chapter Twelve

"Here, have another blanket," River told Hannah, draping yet another heavy blanket around her shoulders as she shivered in front of the fire.

"I'm o-kay," Hannah tried to protest, but her teeth were chattering so much she could hardly get the words out. She clutched the cup of hot cocoa River had made for her and exchanged a glance with Xavier.

They had made it back to the lodge… That was something. The way Xavier was looking at her, though, she could tell it was far from over. Anger was written all over his face, his shoulders hunched up, his fists clenched on his lap. His hair was damp from the warm shower he'd just taken, and he was waiting for Aaron and Bailey to come down to reception so he could fill them in on everything that had happened.

Hannah was still trying to wrap her head around it herself. All of it was such a blur of terror and pain—she wasn't entirely sure how they had made it out, but she knew she had Xavier to thank for it. His calm tone as he had talked her through what he was going to do had been the only thing keeping her grounded. If it hadn't been for him, she was sure she would have drowned in the water that was filling the SUV.

She shivered at the thought. She still didn't know why someone had driven them off the road, but whoever it was had clearly meant them some serious harm. She kept replaying the moment Xavier's vehicle spun off the road, the way time seemed to slow down as it hung in the air, before the sickening thud of it landing in the river below.

Who would have done that to them? And why?

As soon as Xavier and Hannah had stumbled through the lodge doors, everyone in the place sprang into action to take care of them. Lawson had rushed off to find River so she could check them over, and Aaron had gone to get Bailey. She worked for the local police department in Blue Ridge and could take an informal statement to give to Sheriff Willis in the morning.

"Can I have a look at your head now?" River asked gently as she crouched down in front of Hannah.

Hannah nodded, a little worried. She didn't feel too bad, but what if she had a concussion or something?

River ran through a few simple tests, getting Hannah to follow her finger with her eyes, checking out the depth and severity of the wound. Finally she leaned back and nodded. "It doesn't look like it's a concussion," River told her. "Just a cut. I'm going to clean it up and bandage it, okay?"

"Sure," Hannah replied, trying to keep her voice steady. She didn't want anyone to see how shaken she really was, even though she was sure it was obvious.

Xavier reached over to rub her shoulder gently, and she managed to smile at him—God, she was so grateful for everything he had done for her. If it hadn't been for him…

Hannah winced as River cleaned off the cut, then gently placed a bandage over it to keep it from getting infected. She smiled and gave Hannah's hand a squeeze when she was done. "There you go, all finished," she assured her.

Hannah looked toward the front doors as Bailey burst into the reception area, followed closely by Aaron. Lawson and Cade behind them.

"Oh my God," Bailey gasped when she saw Hannah and Xavier. "What happened? Are you okay? Aaron filled me in on some of it, but—"

Xavier gestured for her to take a seat and caught her up on a little of what had happened. He seemed to be able to remember so much more than Hannah did. Her memories were frayed around the edges, and she couldn't piece together everything that had gone down.

Hannah clutched her mug, trying to ignore her brother's heavy gaze, and listened to Xavier speak, trying to let herself be soothed by the sound of his voice. He had made it out okay. They had both made it out okay. That was what mattered right then.

"Do you remember anything specific about the vehicle that hit you?" Bailey asked, pulling out a notebook.

Xavier grimaced. "A little," he admitted. "It was a black truck, looked like a Ford, maybe early 1980s. Custom fog lights and grills."

"Good, good," Bailey muttered, scribbling away in her notebook.

Hannah raised her eyebrows. And that was him only remembering some of it? Damn, he was doing a lot better than her. Thank God he had been there. She wouldn't have been able to give Bailey much more than the color and how terrified she had felt when it was closing in on them.

Aaron shook his head. "I've got a bad feeling about this," he muttered. "Who do you think it was?"

"The Haynes brothers, maybe?" Bailey suggested. "You and Lawson went to their ranch to confront them about the generators. This could have been their way of getting back at you for accusing them."

"I don't think the Haynes family would do something like this," Xavier replied. "They're jerks, sure, but this would have taken some planning—to figure out when we were going to be on the road, finding a place to push us off where nobody else would see. I don't think they've got that in them."

"I agree." Lawson chimed in. "This is not their style."

"Yeah, they've caused a bar fight here and there," Aaron added. "But they've never deliberately endangered lives. This feels more—"

"Personal," Hannah whispered, finishing his sentence for him. The thought of this being a specific, targeted attack scared the hell out of her, more than she could put into words.

"You think it's connected to what happened with the generators?" Bailey asked, continuing to write in her notebook.

"It could be," Xavier agreed, then he hesitated, glancing over at Lawson.

"Tell her," Lawson prompted, realizing what he was about to say.

"Someone broke in to my room a few days ago. I don't think they took anything, but I do think it might be related."

"What?" Bailey replied, looking confused. "I didn't hear about that."

"I hoped there was nothing to it," Xavier admitted. "I just told the sheriff today. That's where we were coming back from when the wreck happened. I should have said something sooner, but I guess I was in denial. This, though…" He shook his head. "Everyone needs to keep their wits about them," he warned the small group. "There's trouble brewing around here. We have to look out for each other."

Silence weighed heavily over everyone for a moment. Hannah knew what was going through their minds—the same thing going through hers. They had been so sure their troubles were over, and now this. A new reason to be scared and watching their backs at all times.

Just when she thought the worst was behind them, something like this sneaked up on them again. The reality of it hurt to think about. This place was supposed to be a safe haven, but instead, someone was intent on tearing it apart and hurting the people who lived and worked there.

"That's enough for now. I'm going to write this all up and you two need to get some rest," Bailey told Xavier, rising to her feet. "And I'll take it to Willis in the morning. He can add it to the file he's building. I don't know what's going on here, but we're going to figure it out, okay?"

Xavier nodded.

Aaron clapped Xavier on the back and followed Bailey back out the door to their cabin.

Silence settled over the remaining group. Hannah could feel Lawson's eyes on her again. She could feel the worry and frustration pouring off him. He'd have questions about her being with Xavier, but she didn't want to address him now.

Hannah was starting to warm up a little, though the

cold that gripped her heart was still sending shivers down her spine.

"You should go to your cabin, too, and get some rest," River told her gently. She took the empty cup from Hannah's hands. "I'll take this back to the kitchen."

"Glad you two are okay." Cade nodded toward them both and followed River down the hallway.

Hannah bit her lip and sighed. She knew River was right, but the thought of trying to sleep after what just happened seemed damn near impossible. How was she supposed to get any rest with everything going on right now…all the possible danger coming their way? Every time she closed her eyes, she had flashbacks of Xavier's SUV flipping off the road into the freezing cold river and being trapped upside down in the rising water. She wasn't sure she would be able to get any rest at all.

Xavier seemed to notice how scared she was, and he reached out for her hand. For a brief moment, the warmth of his skin against hers was enough to ground her, and she looked up at him again.

"You're okay," he promised her. "We're okay. Right?"

"I don't know," she admitted. If there was anyone who could convince her that everything would turn out all right in the end, it was Xavier. He had rescued her from the crash and gotten her out of the water in one piece. He'd carried her up the bank and to the car he had flagged down for them, helped her back to the sanctuary and made sure she was safe and warm.

She felt guilty, almost ungrateful, for feeling as afraid as she did right now, but she couldn't help it. How would she ever be able to rest easy again after what had happened? She felt like it could happen again the next time she got into a vehicle.

"I get that," Xavier assured her. "I know how it feels, when something like this happens. How you can't shut your mind off and stop thinking through the what-ifs."

She chewed her lip. "Does it get better?" she asked softly. She needed to hear it from him. He had always been honest with her, and she knew he would tell her the truth.

He nodded at once. "It does," he promised her. "It really does. You just need to get some rest. I promise it'll start feeling better in the morning, once you've had a good night's sleep."

"I don't know how I'm going to be able to sleep," she admitted as she got to her feet, casting off the blankets River had piled around her. "I feel like I might never sleep again."

"That's the adrenaline," Xavier told her, walking over to her and holding out his hand. Before she could reach for it, her brother appeared at her side.

"Hey, sis. How are you feeling?" Lawson's eyes roamed over her before gently wrapping her in a hug.

Hannah pulled back and gave him a wobbly smile. "I'm tired and achy, worried. But, I'm here. Xavier made sure of that."

Lawson nodded and turned to look between his sister and his best friend.

"So, what were you doing down in town together? I wasn't aware you were leaving the lodge." Lawson inquired, eyebrow raised.

She heard Xavier suck in a breath and her eyes darted quickly to him before back to her brother.

"I ran into Xavier when he was leaving and asked if I could go with him. I just thought the drive would be a nice break. We had lunch after he saw Sheriff Willis, then we came back."

"I see. I thought we talked about this? We discussed—"

"Lawson, can we not do this right now?" Hannah interrupted, wrapping her arms around herself. "Please. It's been a long day and I just want to rest and not think about anything right now."

"Hannah." Lawson sighed and locked his eyes on Xavier for a long moment before turning back to her. "Fine, we'll talk later. I'm glad you're both okay." He shook his head, then turned around and headed across the lobby.

She wasn't ready to leave the warm comfort of the lodge, but she also didn't want to stay and argue with her brother. Her best option right now was her own space. She offered Xavier a small smile and held out her hand. He interlocked their fingers and led her outside.

They walked hand in hand to her cabin, her fingers squeezing his tighter the closer they got. She wasn't ready to be alone yet.

Xavier seemed to since her anxiety.

He brought her hand to his lips and brushed his mouth against it in a soft kiss. "You want me to stay with you tonight?" he murmured.

Relief flooded through her, and she nodded quickly. "Yes," she blurted. "Yes, please. I don't want to be alone."

As he reached for her cabin door, some of the tension she had been carrying was starting to lift slightly. It wasn't much, but it was enough for her to settle her racing heart and take a breath. Maybe she would be able to rest after all.

The adrenaline was starting to fade now, and she could feel the tiredness sweeping through her body. Letting out a yawn, she leaned in to him as he took the key from her, slipping it into the lock.

Xavier pushed the door open and let her inside. "Come on, let's get you settled."

"You want some tea?"

"I'll make it," he replied, guiding her to the small couch in her living room. "You sit down."

She sank into the seat and stole a glance toward the window opposite her. Outside, it seemed as though everything was quiet and still, but she wasn't sure she could believe that. After the fire and then being run off the road, she wasn't sure if she would ever feel safe and secure at Warrior Peak again.

The nagging unease tugged at her stomach, and she tried to ignore it, focusing on the sound of Xavier in the kitchen behind her. As long as he was there with her, everything was going to be all right.

She was sure of it. Right?

# Chapter Thirteen

"Here you go." Xavier handed Hannah a cup of hot chamomile tea as he took a seat next to her on the couch. He took a moment to look her over again, battling both fear and anger at her being caught up in whatever this mess was with him.

It was bad enough that it had started at the lodge, threatening their peace and safety. But then to drag Hannah into it as well, and try to kill them both… He still didn't know if it was coincidence that she happened to be with him when they were run off the road, or if whoever had done this had specifically targeted them both.

She looked a little better since her shower and fresh clothes but fatigue was pulling at her hard, and he could still see the anxiety lurking behind her gaze and the dark circles under her eyes. He was so thankful that they had made it out mostly unscathed. But his eyes caught on the bandage on her forehead and grimaced.

"Does it hurt?" he asked, raising his hand to brush back the hair from her face.

She shook her head. "Not really."

He frowned. She was likely just saying that to keep him from worrying about her. It looked as though it must hurt like hell.

"It's not your fault, Xavier," she reminded him, clearly noticing whatever look was on his face.

He knew she was right, of course, but that didn't stop him from feeling guilty about it. He should have done more to protect her. The fact that she was injured because he hadn't been able to keep her safe didn't sit well with him.

Xavier couldn't help but worry what would happen next. What else would these people try? The thought of it worried him more than he could express.

He was more determined than ever to find out what was going on. He was going to track down whoever was responsible for these things and make them pay. No one messed with Hannah or the lodge on his watch without serious consequences.

"Who do you think it was?" she asked, stealing a glance at him out of the corner of her eye. "I know you told Bailey you weren't sure, but…"

"I have no idea," he admitted with a sigh. "I have to think it has something to do with whoever broke into my room the other night, but that's about as far as I've gotten. I'm not sure what the motive would be for that or for running us off the road."

"Do you have any enemies?" she wondered aloud. "I mean, from your time in the military? Or the CIA?"

"None that I'm aware of," he replied with a shrug. "But they might just have been keeping their heads down until they were able to make their move. I really don't have a clue."

She chewed her lip. That answer didn't seem to be the one she wanted, judging by the troubled look on her face. He guessed she was hoping for something a little more direct, something she could actually work with, but he didn't have anything more for her.

"You know I would tell you if I did, right?" he questioned with one brow raised.

She locked eyes with him and nodded. "I know you would," she agreed, managing a small smile.

She was still seriously shaken, there was no doubt about that, but it meant the world to Xavier that she trusted him and knew that he trusted her as well. He would always be honest with her.

She paused for a moment, blowing on her tea thoughtfully. "Do you think they might have mistaken us for someone else?" she asked hopefully. "Thought someone else was in the vehicle, and that's why they did what they did?"

"It's possible," he replied. Though he didn't think that was very likely. It would have been a relief if this was a case of mistaken identity, but it would still leave unanswered the questions of the damaged generators and who had been rummaging through his stuff.

"But you don't think so?" she prompted him, able to read his face just like always.

He sighed. "I don't think so," he admitted. "I don't think someone who came after us with that much anger would mistake us for anyone else. I think it was about… about me."

His voice cracked. He wished he didn't have to come to terms with that part. He didn't want to acknowledge that he had been the one to pull her into this, to put her in danger. He was the reason she was sitting there with a bandage on her head, in pain and afraid to be alone.

She widened her eyes, and they started to gloss with tears. From fear? For him or for her or maybe for both?

Xavier would never forgive himself if something happened to Warrior Peak or any of its employees or guests because of some vendetta a person he didn't even know had against him. Let alone if something happened to Hannah as a result.

"What happens if they come after you again?" she asked, her voice taking on an edge of panic. "They're going to escalate, right?"

"They might," he agreed. Truthfully, he didn't even want to think about how far they would take it. Not because he was worried about himself—he knew how to handle anything the world threw at him. He had learned that from his time in the military and the CIA. Nobody would outsmart him. Nobody who didn't have those skills themselves, at least.

"What's going to happen to you?" she whispered, as though she hardly dared to consider the possibility of it.

"Nothing will," he promised. "You don't have to worry about me. Whoever is doing these things, they don't know who they're dealing with. I'll figure this out, and I'll handle it." He reached over and gave her hand a squeeze. "But I... I'm not sure if you should be around me right now, Hannah."

She stared at him, and for a moment, she looked so small and vulnerable, it made his chest hurt.

He wanted to be close to her, of course he did. He wanted to keep her by his side to protect her, but after what had happened today, he was worried what that closeness might cost her. He was already beating himself up about her being with him on the road and the attack. His gut tightened at the thought of anything worse happening as a result of her being with him.

"What do you mean?" she asked, her voice quivering.

"I don't know who's after me," he confessed. "But after today, I know they're willing to go pretty damn far to try to hurt me or get my attention. And if they know how much I care about you, it could put you in danger, too."

She sat there for a moment, taking in what he had just. A tear rolled down her cheek, but she wiped it away quickly and lifted the tea to her lips to take a sip. "I don't care about that," she said at last.

"Hannah, you can't say that—"

"Yes, I can," she replied firmly, shaking her head. "Listen to me, Xavier. I know you're trying to protect me, I get that, and I appreciate it. But… I care about you. I have for a long time now."

He gave her a small smile at her confession. There was really no reason for either of them to deny their feelings at this point. It was written all over their faces when they were around each other anyway.

"I'm not going to let these people scare me away from what I want. What I need," she continued, reaching out for his hand, her small fingers wrapping around his. "I can't lose you. I've waited too long for this. The way you kissed me in town today, I… It was everything I've been waiting for. Everything I've been too scared to hope for. I'm not letting it slip through my fingers again, not a chance in hell."

He couldn't speak, just rubbing his thumb along her knuckles as he listened to her. He should have cut her off before this went any further, but he just didn't have it in him to stop this, not when her words were everything he had been craving, too.

"I want…us. Together. I want you, Xavier," she confessed. "The waiting and hoping and holding back and pretending I don't feel the way I do… It's been killing me. I don't care what I have to deal with to be with you. I want you. I want us. And if you can't handle that, I need you to tell me now." Her voice was taut, but her words were firm.

His eyes searched hers, doubtful. He wanted her, more than anything. The thought of more harm coming to her, especially because of him, was almost more than he could bear. "You could get hurt again," he warned her with narrowed eyes.

She smiled. "I could get hurt again," she repeated. "But if you break this off now, I *am* going to get hurt. No doubt about it. And I can handle it, if that's what you really want. But I… I think you want this as much as I do."

His head warred with his heart as he took in her words. Of course he wanted to be with her. He had dreamed of being with her for so long, it was almost too much to hope for. He craved that more than anything in the world, even more than finding out who had done all these things to Warrior Peak. He needed her. There'd always been a place deep down inside of him that called out for her.

He reached out to caress her face, and she closed her eyes and rested her head in his hand. Even a simple touch like this told him what he wanted. No matter what the risk was, he had to have her. There had always been something in their way, something pushing the two of them apart, but he was well and truly done with it now. Whether it was her brother, his PTSD, or whatever outside threat was bearing down on them, he was finished with it. He couldn't let it stop him from being with the woman he loved.

He leaned in and planted a kiss against her lips, his voice fierce when he spoke again.

"That kiss today was the best thing that's happened to me in a long time," he murmured to her. "I want you, Hannah. I want us to be together."

She smiled, looping her arms around his shoulders.

As he gazed into her eyes, he was struck by her strength and determination, yet at the same time her fragility underneath it all. How much of his own pain and suffering would bleed on to her if he didn't do something to deal with his past? He had avoided getting help for his PTSD and nightmares for so damn long, but maybe this was the push he needed to finally deal with them—to finally start addressing all that pain he had hoped would just fade on its own.

He swore to himself, in that moment, that he would do whatever it took to keep her safe. Not just from whoever was targeting them but from himself, too. He wasn't going to let her suffer from the trauma that he still carried with him. The first chance he got, he was going to go to Sarah and tell her that he needed her help. God only knew how true that was, no matter how much he had tried to deny it. He was ready to move forward.

Hannah kissed him again, this time, a little more intention behind her touch. She knew as well as he did that they couldn't deny what they felt for each other any longer. Regardless of her brother or whoever else might stand in their way, they were meant to be together. Maybe life would have been simpler if they could resist, but now there was nothing left to do but give in to the feelings they'd denied for so long.

He didn't need to say the words, but he was sure she felt them, too, as their kiss deepened. He drew her into his lap, needing her closer. He wasn't sure if he would ever get close enough to her, if the need that had throbbed inside of him for so long would ever be sated.

He could no longer deny his true feelings or his desire to be with her.

He was in this. They were in this.

Whatever happened going forward, they would be together.

## *Chapter Fourteen*

Hannah slowly came to, and the sensation of a weight in bed next to her drew her attention. Her head hurt, but she could hardly pay attention to it as she glanced over at the other side of the bed. Then she buried her face into the pillow to hide her grin.

Xavier. He was right there next to her. Last night had been amazing. It was the first time they had truly come together in the way she had fantasized about for so long, and it had been *good*. Way better than even her wildest fantasies were able to prepare her for. His touch was so strong, so effortless—the way he kissed her, the way he held her, the way he looked at her—it made her head spin with the most delicious pleasure she had ever experienced.

And now, here he was, sleeping next to her. He was lying on his side facing her so, she reached her arm out over his chest tentatively, not wanting to wake him up. She was sure he needed his sleep as much as she did right now, and she didn't intend to disturb him. She lightly brushed her hand along his strong chest, marveling at how good it felt, and an excited little giggle bubbled up in her throat. After all this time, all this waiting, it felt wonderful to finally have him there with her.

Snuggling against him, she flipped over so that her

back was pressed against his chest. He wrapped his arm around her waist almost on instinct and pulled her closer.

Hannah closed her eyes, savoring the feeling and wanting nothing more than to doze off again. She was sure there were plenty of tasks she needed to do today, but the only thing she cared about right then was resting up and feeling the warm comfort of him close to her.

She was just starting to fall asleep once more, feeling the faint sensation of his heartbeat against her back, when suddenly, something shifted.

His arm constricted around her all of a sudden, gripping on to her like he didn't want to let go. His breath was coming harder and faster, but not like it had when they were intimate the night before. This felt like something else entirely.

Hannah wiggled to get a little more room between them, then she drew herself back and slowly turned to face him.

His eyes were open but unfocused. He was looking at her but not seeing her. His body was stiff and twitching slightly, as though he was in the middle of some deadly battle right there in his mind.

"Xavier?" she whispered to him nervously, but it didn't draw a response. He was dreaming. This must be one of the nightmares he'd told her about. Seeing him in the midst of it, and not knowing how to help him, hurt her heart. This was far different than what she'd thought it would be like.

His hands bunched up the covers, and his body jerked sharply, then contorted like he was in pain, before straightening out again.

She lifted her hand and waved it a couple of times in

front of his face, but there was no response. She had never seen anyone in this state of distress before, and she wasn't sure of what to do. Her heart clenched at the thought of him reliving this terrible pain. She felt all but helpless.

His lips parted, and he croaked out a word. Over and over again, his voice so low and muffled she could hardly make it out.

She shifted a little closer to him, making sure not to touch him, trying to understand what he was saying.

*Max*.

He was saying his brother's name. Chanting it almost as though it was some kind of spell that would bring him back to life.

Tears sprang to her eyes at the thought of what he must be seeing in his dream. Was this what it was like every night for him? Remembering that one battle that took his brother's life over and over again? Hannah wished she knew what was going on inside his head, but the best she could do was try to pull him out of the memory as safely as possible.

Sarah had talked her through it before, the basics of how to pull someone out of a flashback like this. She had suggested it would be a good idea with the guests they catered to, just in case Hannah was around when someone had an episode and needed assistance. It would save time rather than trying to find another person to help.

Hannah wasn't sure if the same thing would apply for a dream, but it was all she knew to try. She didn't want to call someone else, knowing that Xavier wouldn't want anyone seeing him in this vulnerable state.

She sat up and moved back some to give him a little more space, suddenly distinctly aware of just how powerful Xavier was—how strong and lethal he could be. Not that he would ever have used that against her willingly, when he was awake and conscious of his actions. But right now, he was definitely *not* awake, so she needed to be damn careful about how she approached this.

"Xavier," she spoke his name quietly, not wanting to suddenly shock him into wakefulness.

He was still mumbling rapidly under his breath, his eyes sliding sightlessly back and forth as he witnessed who knew what horrors inside his head.

She knew she couldn't stop them entirely, but she could at least try to pull him out of this and bring him back to the real world, remind him that he was safe, with her in her cabin, in her bed. She didn't want his first night staying with her to be marred with these memories.

She took a calming breath before speaking to him again. "Xavier, can you hear me?" she asked gently but firmly. She wanted to reach out and touch him, but she knew it might trigger a more violent response. In his addled state, he might think someone was attacking him and lash out. She wished she could just take his hand and give it a tight squeeze or give him a big hug and make all of this go away, but she had to be smart and help him the right way.

She had to show him that she was capable of handling whatever came with being with him—even when it was scary or tough.

"Xavier, I don't know what's going through your head right now," she continued softly. "But I need you to know that you're safe. Okay? You're in my cabin. You're in my bed. This is Hannah, and I'm here to help you through this."

For a moment, his mumbling stopped, like he could actually hear her. She continued talking, repeating what she had just said again. She spoke slowly and clearly, even though inside, her heart was breaking at the sight of him like this. Realizing that he'd been struggling with these nightmares all this time, she just couldn't wrap her head around it. To think he was doing this all alone, with no one there to pull him back. It wasn't right.

She was never going to let him deal with them alone again.

The third time she repeated herself, something seemed to shift in him. His breathing began to slow and level out, and his eyes drifted shut once more. The grip he'd had on the covers loosened slightly, and he let out a long, shaky breath.

"Xavier?" Hannah murmured, still a little wary. Had she done the right thing? Perhaps she should have gone up to the lodge and got proper help for him. Wake up Sarah, or even her brother. Lawson would have some words about Xavier being in her bed, but she knew he'd help his best friend. Either one of them would be more equipped to deal with this situation.

But then, Xavier's eyes opened once more. They flitted around the room before settling on Hannah. He wiped away the sheen of sweat on his forehead and then reached out to take her hand. "Hannah?" he muttered. His voice was hoarse and quiet, but he was here—he was back with her, not lost to that nightmare that had just consumed him.

She breathed a sigh of relief. "Yeah, it's me," she told him, squeezing his hand. "Are you...are you okay?"

He paused before he replied, and she knew the answer before he spoke it out loud. Of course he wasn't okay. How the hell could he be? Whatever he had just been through, it had been really bad. Even last night, faced with the car crash and having to find a way out of the sinking SUV, he hadn't looked as shaken as he was right now.

She hated seeing him like this, but the fact that he didn't feel the need to hide it from her felt like a big shift. A huge relief.

"No, not really," he replied. "I'm sorry. Did I wake you?"

She shook her head. "I was already up," she assured him. "I saw there was something wrong. Do you...do you have nightmares like this a lot?"

"Usually worse," he admitted.

Her eyes widened. Worse? How could they be worse than that?

"I'm sorry," he murmured again.

She gripped his hand a little tighter. "You have nothing to be sorry for," she promised him. "I—I knew things were bad, but I didn't realize just how bad they were for you. This has been happening for a while now?"

"Since the fire," he replied with a sigh, propping himself up. He still seemed a little off, as though he was still shaking off the remnants of the nightmare.

She thought, for a moment, about asking him what he had dreamed about but quickly decided against it. As curious as she was, she didn't want to ask him to go through those memories again, especially when they were still so fresh in his mind. The best thing she could do was show him support, let him know she was there for him and encourage him to get proper help.

"I'm sorry you're having to deal with that. I do hope you'll reconsider talking to Sarah about them," she added gently. He had seemed resistant to it before, but a lot had changed since then. Between them, especially. She hoped it would be enough for him to stop denying himself the help he so clearly needed.

"Yeah, I am," he replied. "I don't even know where to start, though."

"You don't need to know where to start," she reminded him. "That's what she's there for. She'll know how to sort through all of this way better than either of us could."

He nodded but then offered her a smile. "I think you did a pretty damn good job there," he remarked.

She glanced away from him, shaking her head. "Oh, I just did what anyone would do."

"You did amazing," he replied firmly. "I don't know many people who could pull someone out of a flashback like that, especially without some form of training."

"Sarah offered to guide me through the basics a while back. Thought it would be good to know working here. Never thought I'd have to try it out."

"You handled it just fine. You didn't panic or get frustrated or overreact," he pointed out. "You shouldn't downplay it, Hannah. You should be proud of yourself. I sure am. I would be doing a lot worse right now if it wasn't for you. I'm usually a whole lot more stressed and anxious when I come out of a nightmare."

He pulled her to him, and she snuggled against his chest, grateful for their closeness once more. His presence next to her was everything she needed right now, even if she could still feel some of the tension in his body from that nightmare he'd just had.

And she knew it wouldn't be the last time she would have to talk him down from one of those flashbacks. It didn't work that way. No matter how much better things seemed to be between them now, how much closer they'd become after sharing their feelings for each other.

Healing wouldn't happen immediately; it would take time and proper therapy for him. At least he was willing and ready to try, and she'd be there for him in whatever capacity she could be to help him through it.

She wanted Xavier no matter what he was dealing with; wanted to be with him fully and completely. She wanted to be with him as he healed, to see him grow and change into the man he wanted and deserved to be. The man who was free from the pain and guilt he had carried around for so long. She didn't want him to live in the past and suffer over and over again, reliving his brother's death.

Hannah closed her eyes and nestled against him, breathing in his scent. She was so thankful that they had finally been open and honest about their feelings. And that they were together. Despite the stress of the nightmare, she was content and happy.

He pushed a hand through her hair and kissed her temple, and she smiled against his chest. Yeah, she might just stay in bed a little longer yet.

# *Chapter Fifteen*

Xavier shifted in the chair. He wasn't sure why, but he didn't like the feel of it. It was comfortable, almost too comfortable, like it would have been all too easy to just sink in to the soft fabric and never get out. He had already pulled off all the pillows and piled them on the floor in front of him when Sarah had told him to arrange the room however he felt most at ease, and he was sure she already thought he was crazy for that.

She offered him a smile from the large, heavy chair she sat in opposite him.

He never imagined that he would find himself here, of all places. He never thought he would be in therapy talking about his feelings and sharing his innermost thoughts. When they hired Sarah, it had been for her to take care of the guests at the lodge, not one of the owners. But he knew, clearer than ever, how much he needed this help, even if he was having a hard time figuring out how to start the conversation.

Seeing the look on Hannah's face when he woke up from that flashback had been enough to make him certain he needed to be here. He couldn't keep putting her through having to help him out of his nightmares or possibly even put her in danger from them. It wasn't fair to her or their newfound relationship. He felt bad enough that she'd witnessed the one she did.

She'd handled the situation well and had done a good job of bringing him back to the present, but he didn't want to be a burden on her or their relationship in that way. He wanted to be her partner, not have her see him as someone broken and reliant on her for help every time he had a nightmare. If they were going to be together, he needed to embrace these head-on and get the help he'd needed for a while now.

And Sarah was offering him a chance to do that. Beside her, on the desk, a small diffuser puffed out scented steam. It smelled like the vapor rub his mother used to put on his chest when he had a cold—menthol and medicinal. Sarah had a notepad sitting just next to her and a pen ready to jot down any observations she might make on what he had to say.

For some reason, this made him uncomfortable—talking about it was one thing, but having it written down and made permanent? That was something else entirely. It made him feel more vulnerable. Exposed in a way he didn't like at all.

"So," Sarah began as the silence hung heavy in the room between them, "I'm really glad you came to speak to me today, Xavier."

He grunted his acknowledgment and shifted in his chair. He was uncomfortable with the thought of spilling his guts to this woman. He'd never told anyone the specifics of the nightmares he'd been dealing with. Not even his best friend and business partner, Lawson, knew the full extent—just what little he'd shared after Max's death since Lawson had been there at that time to offer his support. And Hannah only knew what little she'd witnessed.

He never liked burdening people with what he was going through, but right now, he didn't have a choice. He knew he just had to push himself to get started, but he couldn't find the right words to say what he wanted to.

"You mentioned to me before that you'd received a diagnosis of PTSD from a previous physician, is that right?" Sarah asked.

"I had to see someone before I started working for the CIA," he explained. "That's what he told me it was. Never put much stock in it, until…" He trailed off, tripping over his words again. He wasn't used to talking about any of this, and his instincts were screaming for him to stop. He'd dealt with his nightmares on his own for so long, it seemed unnatural to share his troubles with someone else.

"Until?" she prompted him.

He shook his head.

"It's okay," she assured him. "You don't have to talk about anything you're not ready to. I just want to get a general idea of how you're doing and where you're at with your mental health. Do you mind if I ask a few questions?"

He gestured for her to keep talking, wishing he could pull himself together. It felt like he was stepping in the silt of his memories, all those parts of himself that he had tried to leave behind pressing up against him once more. How could he just talk about it? Say it out loud, when he still felt so much guilt and shame for what he had done?

Or, more accurate, what he had failed to do?

"We didn't talk much about your diagnosis before," she continued, jotting something down on her notepad.

"But I've heard from Lawson that you've been struggling with nightmares recently."

Lawson. Of course he had talked to her about it. Xavier shook his head slightly. "He's been talking to you about it?"

"Nothing specific, but yes, he has," she replied. "Your friends are concerned about you, Xavier. They want the best for you."

He sighed. "I'm concerned, too," he admitted finally, picking at a loose thread on the chair beneath him. "I... I thought these nightmares were over, you know? I had them a lot right after I got back from overseas, but they started to fade after a while. I would still have these memories, but when I would wake up, I knew it was a dream, and I could bring myself back to reality pretty easily."

"And you've been having more trouble with that recently?" Sarah asked.

He nodded again. "Yeah, it feels like I'm right back there, all over again," he continued, his voice lowering. He was going to need to get used to talking to her like this; hopefully, it would get easier over time. "Like I'm watching my brother die all over again," he added.

He hated saying those words out loud. Acknowledging that Max was gone hurt in a way nothing else did—a permanent wound that would never heal, a reminder of how much he had failed his little brother. He had promised his mother he would do everything he could to keep him safe, but when it came down to it, he had failed. He knew he was never going to be able to forgive himself for that.

Sarah frowned, nodding kindly.

He averted his eyes to stare at the floor. What must she think of him, a man who failed to keep his own brother safe? He didn't even want to know. Logically, of course he understood that she had heard far worse things in her time here at Warrior Peak. He still felt like she would never look at him the same way again.

"It's really common to face a setback in your recovery after a traumatic event," she explained.

Xavier shook his head. "I haven't had a traumatic event." Not by his standards, anyway. Yeah, the fire wasn't exactly pleasant, but he had seen far worse in his time. He felt like he would have sounded crazy to compare that to what he'd endured in the service.

"The fire?" Sarah prompted him. "Isn't that when these dreams really started to cause you problems again?"

He nodded.

"I understand that you may not have felt traumatized by the fire, but chances are that it triggered your fight-or-flight response," she explained. "It's a method the nervous system uses to handle particularly threatening or dangerous situations, whether they're actually bad news or just perceived by your brain as such. Does that make sense?"

He shrugged. "Yeah, I guess." He didn't feel like he had any right to make the attack on the sanctuary about him. Everyone had felt the danger and struggled that night.

"And it seems like your brain has interpreted that as being back in the midst of the event that caused you the most trauma," she continued. "That's why the dreams have been coming up again. Your brain is trying to warn and protect you, even though there's nothing like that going on right now."

*Like that.* She was careful to phrase it that way. She knew there was something going on around here, just like

Xavier did. Could he really put this work into recovery, when he was sure there were people after him right now? He shifted in his seat again, not speaking.

"And what I want to do with these sessions is teach your brain that those memories are in the past, they're not happening now, and that you're safe," she continued. "I understand how hard that must seem to you, but it is possible. Lots of people suffer trauma as a result of being involved in combat, and it's really common to deal with PTSD and nightmares in the aftermath. But it doesn't have to stay that way, okay? You don't have to deal with this alone."

He could feel a well of emotion rising up in him, and he tried to push it down.

"Your friends here really care about you," Sarah went on. "I do, too. I've seen all the great work you've done here, all the ways you've created a safe space for the people who've been through what you have, and you deserve to give that kindness to yourself, too. Do you think you can do that?"

"I don't know," he admitted. Faced with the choice, there was a part of him that wanted to push back and deny himself what he knew he needed. But then, he closed his eyes, and he thought of Hannah. He thought of her lying beside him in bed, her eyes wide as she tried to pull him from the horrors in his head.

And he knew he had to try. He couldn't keep pretending this wasn't happening. He had tried that already, and he was pretty damn clear on the fact that it hadn't worked. His eyes were fixed on the diffuser beside her, and he tried to time his breath to the sound of its low hum. Anything to ground himself, to pull him into this moment instead of dealing with the usual fight that boiled in his system when he was faced with telling the truth about how he felt and what he had been through.

"Yes, I do," he corrected himself finally. "I… I want to try. I don't know how, but I want to try."

A warm, genuine smile lit up Sarah's entire face. "I'm so glad to hear that," she gushed, and she reached over to pull her notepad into her lap. "And you don't need to know how—that's what I'm here for."

He nodded. He had to let her take the lead. It was fine for him not to know what he was doing here. That was why he had come in the first place.

"So, let's start by going through the content of these dreams," she prompted him. "Do you think you can manage that?"

He gritted his teeth, fighting the usual urge to just close off as soon as anyone asked him about that time in his life. But finally, he spoke. "They all start the same way. My brother and I are under fire…"

# Chapter Sixteen

"Uh, do you have the manual there?" Hannah called to River, as she carried over an armful of lightbulbs, stakes and a couple boxes of screws.

"I think Bailey has it on her phone," River called back, pulling a face as she reached Hannah. "It's one of those downloadable ones."

"Oh, they're the worst." Hannah sighed. "Why can't they put a paper manual in the box?"

"My thoughts exactly," Bailey cut in as she followed River out of the main entrance to the lodge.

"I printed it out. Here, let's see where we need to get started." Bailey appeared from behind them.

Hannah grinned as the women joined her along the edge of the path they were working on today. Together, they were setting up some solar-powered lights that would lead the way through the darkness if there were any issues with the generators again. It had been River's idea, and Hannah had agreed to help her at once. After the tumble she'd taken, even though it just scraped up her knees, she didn't want anyone else to possibly come to harm if the power went out again.

None of them really knew what they were doing, but between the three of them, she knew they'd figure it all

out and get them working in no time. She had been working and living alongside River and Bailey for months now,
and having the women around felt like second nature to
her. They had become close in their time together, and
though Hannah knew eventually they would likely move
on to other things, she was glad for their company.

Especially now. It had been nearly a week since she
and Xavier had been driven off the road, and she was still
trying to wrap her head around it. They were no closer
to finding out who might have done it or why. And it
had left Hannah feeling spooked and worried. She was
looking over her shoulder all the time now, waiting for
something else to happen, worried she wouldn't be able
to stop it if it did.

Putting in the solar lights was as much an attempt to
get her mind on to something more useful as it was to
make a difference around the lodge, and River seemed
to know that Hannah needed something to distract her.

As they laid out their tools and started to read through
the instructions, River glanced over at Hannah, a concerned expression on her face. "You all right?" she murmured quietly.

Hannah sighed. River was perceptive when it came to
people's emotions, and it was clear she had good reason
to be concerned about Hannah.

Hannah shook her head. "Not really," she admitted.
"I… These last few days have just been a lot, that's all."

"I can imagine," River agreed as Bailey dropped the
instructions and joined the conversation.

"We're doing everything we can to get to the bottom
of it," Bailey assured her.

Hannah managed to smile at her. "Yeah, I know," she

replied. "And I appreciate it, I really do. It's just that...
Well, it's not just me I'm worried about."

"Oh?" River prompted her, curious.

"No. Xavier, too," Hannah admitted. "He's been having these...nightmares. I think what happened to us out on the road is really getting to him. I just wish there was more that I could do to help."

River and Bailey exchanged a glance, and Bailey cocked an eyebrow. "Nightmares?"

"Yeah, there's just been a lot going on lately. Between the recent fire, the generators and then the crash..." Hannah trailed off, trying to answer without divulging details. She knew that the others there at the sanctuary knew Xavier had troubles in his past, but it wasn't her story to share. If he wanted everyone to know the particulars, that was his choice. She wasn't going to break his trust in her. "He just feels responsible for everyone here, you know?"

"Understandable. So, that's why he's been seeing Sarah?" River asked.

"River!" Bailey protested her nosiness. "That's not our business."

"No, that's okay," Hannah tried to ease the rising tension. "It's just not for me to discuss. I've been trying to help, but I can only do so much."

"That explains the nightly visits, then." Bailey waggled her eyebrows at Hannah.

"Bailey!" River scolded her in return. "That's not the issue here."

Hannah snort-laughed at them both under her breath. She reminded herself that they wouldn't be so nosy if they didn't care about her and Xavier.

"Hey, I'm just saying, I've seen Xavier come out of

your cabin every day this week," Bailey replied, holding her hands up. "I wondered if that meant the two of you had finally done something about...well, the obvious."

"What's obvious?" Hannah asked, but she couldn't help but crack a smile.

"How much the two of you like each other," Bailey explained. "I mean, it's written all over your faces whenever the two of you are together."

"Is it?" Hannah replied, laughing.

"Yeah, come on, even Lawson can tell," River pointed out.

Hannah glanced back toward the lodge building. Yeah, she had to assume that her brother had figured out what was going on between Xavier and her.

After the crash, Lawson had tried to talk to her, but she'd shut him down and then left with Xavier. So, even if he didn't know specifics, he had to suspect. But, surprisingly, he hadn't confronted her yet. She hoped to keep it that way for a bit longer, they all had enough to worry about right now.

"I think we're giving it a real shot this time," Hannah confessed.

River reached out to give her arm an excited squeeze. "Oh, I'm so happy for you guys," she gushed.

Bailey chuckled. "Plus, I think that means I've won the betting pool," she added.

Hannah's eyebrows shot up. "The betting pool? On when we were going to get together? Don't tell me that was a real thing!"

"It isn't," River assured her. "We're just happy for you, that's all. The two of you deserve it."

"Thanks," Hannah replied. She felt her cheeks get

warm from all this attention, but honestly, it felt good to share how thrilled she was about what they had going on. It had been crazy, these last few months, but if there was one thing she was sure of among all of the madness, it was him.

It had always been him.

"Anyway, we need to get these lights set up," Bailey announced, crouching down on her haunches and grabbing a screwdriver. "River, can you hold this in place while I screw it in?"

"Oh, why don't you get Hannah to do that?" River joked. "She's the expert after all."

"Huh—hey!" Hannah's cheeks warmed as she protested, and all three women burst out laughing.

Hannah could already feel herself starting to relax, starting to believe that everything was actually going to be okay. No matter what the outside world threw at them, Warrior Peak had a solid base of people who pulled together when they needed each other most, and she was beyond grateful that she was a part of it. They set to work putting together the lights. It was a pleasant day, one of the first of the year, with the sun attempting to peep out from behind some clouds.

It took a few attempts to get the lights right. Hannah managed to put the first one in back to front, and they had to take it apart and start all over again, but soon, they got into a pace and had almost filled one side of the path with new lighting. As Hannah straightened up to catch her breath, she noticed someone wandering out of the main entrance. And as soon as she saw who it was, she felt herself tense.

Jed. She'd almost forgotten about him in the midst

of everything else. She wasn't sure what it was about him, but there was a part of her that really didn't like the way he strolled about this place. She had tried to brush it off as best she could, not wanting to assume anything about a man she hardly knew, but it was getting harder and harder to ignore. Most of the people here kept their heads down and focused on themselves when they first arrived, but he seemed intent on garnering the attention of anyone he was able to.

He made his way over to the women and greeted Hannah with a nod. "How's your head?" he asked, smirking as he gestured toward the bandage still covering the wound from the accident.

She reached up to touch it—she had almost forgotten it was there. "It's getting better, thanks," she replied. "How are you doing?"

"Good," he responded, that too-easy smile covering his face again as he looked between the three women. "It's starting to feel like home here. Fresh air, good food. And when you've got a therapist who looks like *that*, how can you complain, right?"

He laughed, but none of the women did.

Hannah stared at him, a sinking feeling in the pit of her stomach. How could he talk about Sarah like that? She was amazing at her job. And yeah, she was beautiful, but it had nothing to do with the relationship she had with her clients. Hearing him speak about her in that way…it didn't sit right with her.

"Anyway, I'll leave you ladies to it," he remarked, and he headed down toward the cabin he was staying in.

Hannah waited until he was out of earshot. "Well, that was gross and uncalled for."

"Wasn't it?" Bailey agreed. "Why is he talking about Sarah like that? And to us."

"He gives me the creeps," River added. "I don't like him. I haven't liked him since he got here. It seems as if he's just lurking around sometimes. Watching."

"Really?" Hannah replied, relieved. So, it wasn't just her who had noticed how off he seemed. It wasn't that he acted less nervous or insecure than most of the other guests. While he did seem cockier and more self-assured, that didn't necessarily bother her. It probably wouldn't have even stood out to her at all if it were anyone else.

"Yeah, I noticed him standing off path the other day, kind of back in the trees. Like he was watching something, or waiting. When he saw me, he turned around pretty quickly and walked off. It was weird."

Hannah and Bailey exchanged a worried look at River's words.

"Cade thought something seemed off about him, too," River added. "The more I see of him, the more I think he was right to have his doubts about him. I definitely don't want to be alone with him."

"I haven't seen a whole lot of him," Bailey interjected. "But if you guys think there might be a problem there, I'll speak to Aaron about it and see if there's anything he can do to keep a closer eye on him."

Hannah felt a little guilty for even considering speaking to Xavier about this, but at the same time, she didn't want to ignore what might end up being a problem. If she had learned anything these last few months, it was not to brush aside the emotions that she didn't want to deal with. Good or bad, she needed to deal with them and share her thoughts when something was bothering her.

There was no harm in the three of them being cautious and watching their step around the guy, right? If there was truly nothing going on, then there was no harm in just asking the guys to keep an eye on him for a while.

"I'll speak to Xavier about him, too," Hannah added, deciding that she needed to say something.

She didn't want to divide Xavier's focus any further right now or give him more to be concerned about, but at the same time, if there was something worrisome going on around the sanctuary, he would want to know about it. He was part owner, after all, and he and Lawson worked hard to keep out trouble and give their guests a safe place to recover. He wouldn't want anybody there feeling uncomfortable or threatened in any way by another guest.

Jed was probably less careful about what he said to the women, and he might put up a front when it came to the guys so they didn't get suspicious or look any further into his reasons for being there.

"Guess we should get back to work," Bailey remarked, gesturing to all the lights that still needed to be put into place.

Hannah nodded in agreement and tried to push the comment Jed had made about Sarah to the back of her mind. But it troubled her. There was something off about that guy. And she needed to find out what it was before anything came of it.

## Chapter Seventeen

As Xavier tightened the last screw into place, he took a step back to admire his handiwork on the latest addition to the lodge building.

"Pretty impressive, if I do say so myself," Aaron remarked, grinning. "Though I still don't know why anyone would want to jump into freezing cold water first thing in the morning."

"Hey, if it helps them, that's what matters," Xavier pointed out. He dusted off his hands and reached for the half-full cup of coffee he'd been sipping on to help motivate him through the construction.

The cold plunge tub had been Lawson's idea, after he heard about it helping athletes in their recovery. He'd done a little research into it and found that it had some decent therapeutic value for people dealing with trauma, the shock of the cold sometimes enough to pull them out of a flashback. He wouldn't say anything to the others about it, but he could attest to the accuracy from his icy showers when he needed the extra help coming back to reality.

And besides, there was still plenty of work to do before it was ready to go. Aaron had offered to give him a hand putting it together, and they were making good progress. Plus, it was a distraction from Xavier's meeting with Sarah in a bit, though he realized that he didn't feel the usual dread when he thought about seeing her. He was starting to get used to their meetings, even if he still came out of them feeling drained.

Slowly, he could feel himself starting to open up. Beyond just the question-and-answer sessions they had with her pulling information out of him, he was freely volunteering stuff to her now, glad to get it off his chest after so long holding it back. There were still so many painful memories to go through. He hadn't even really talked much to her about how his family had reacted after he had returned from service without his brother in tow, but he was getting somewhere.

The nightmares had still been pretty bad, but he figured that was a given, at least for the time being, as he brought up all these painful memories again. He was actually beginning to think they'd get easier, lessen in time. Sarah had already given him a few skills to help manage the immediate aftermath of his dreams when he woke up—grounding techniques to keep him from spinning out of control and to remind him where he was and that he was safe here.

And more than anything, he could tell how happy it made Hannah, which was reason enough to keep going. When Xavier struggled with motivation, he would just look at her and remind himself why he was doing this in the first place: to become the kind of man she deserved—without worry, without doubt, without second-guessing herself for being with him.

It wasn't her job to put those pieces of him back together and he didn't want to become a burden or a regret for her. It was his responsibility to fix himself, to do the work and put in the time to be whole again. He had to want to be whole again. And thanks to Hannah, he did.

Just as Xavier was about to put down his now empty coffee mug and get back to the cold plunge tub, Aaron brought up something that made him stop in his tracks.

"You know what Bailey said to me yesterday?" he asked.

Xavier raised his eyebrows at him. "No idea."

"She told me to keep an eye on that Jed guy," he replied, frowning.

Xavier paused. He'd had a similar conversation with Hannah the night before, too. She had tried to make it sound as casual as possible, but he could tell from her expressions and body language just how much it bothered her. Jed had said some stuff to the women, she'd told him, that had given them reason to wonder if his motivations for being at the sanctuary were entirely pure. She wouldn't go into the details, but she just asked Xavier to look out for Jed to see if there was anything strange that he noticed about him, too.

"What did she say?" Xavier asked. Had the women been talking about him among themselves or had they all just overheard him make a few off comments and wanted to do something about it? Either way, his ears perked up. He knew how guys could be when they thought there was nobody important listening. Unfortunately, for some men, *nobody important* included women.

"Apparently, she was helping Hannah and River put up lights outside and he approached them and made a comment about Sarah. It had them wondering why he was really here," Aaron explained. "Bailey hadn't really had contact with Jed before that, but she said Hannah and River were uncomfortable around him."

"Hannah mentioned something similar to me. She doesn't really think he fits here, like he's putting up a fake front for some reason. What do you think of him?" Xavier asked, his eyebrows drawing together.

"I haven't spent much time with the guy either," he admitted. "I've seen him standing around some outside, not talking to anyone, just looking around. But nothing to make me think something was going on." Aaron shrugged. "However, River and Hannah are around the guests more than we are, so if they feel something's not quite right, I'm inclined to believe them. What about you?"

Xavier sighed. "I don't know, I haven't really been around him either. I met him when he arrived and he recognized me as an owner, which I have to admit was odd. That's not something we advertise outright," he answered thoughtfully.

"If the women are worried enough to bring it to our attention, we need to mention it to Cade and Lawson."

"River told Hannah that Cade's already aware. I'll bring it up to Lawson when I see him later."

Aaron nodded. "Sounds good. We all need to be alert."

"When I first saw him, I thought maybe I knew him from somewhere. He had a familiar 'feel' to him. He kind of reminded me of my brother."

Aaron cocked his head. "Your brother?"

"Max," Xavier replied. It felt strange to say his name out loud after holding it in for so long. "The look in his eyes, the way he carried himself."

Aaron nodded again, waiting for Xavier to continue.

Xavier could tell that Aaron knew how big of a deal it was for him to bring up his brother like that out of nowhere. It wouldn't have surprised Xavier if Lawson had mentioned Max to Aaron and filled him in on everything that had happened to allow Xavier's family ranch to fall into their hands, leading them to create Warrior Peak Sanctuary in the first place.

It used to hurt to even think of him. And there was still a deep, raw sadness when Xavier considered the fact his brother was gone—really, truly gone. But he couldn't keep hiding from it for the rest of his life, no matter how tempting it might have been. He was ready to face it. To talk about him, to remember more than just the last few brutal moments of his existence. Max had been so much more than his death, and Xavier was making a point to try to put that first in his mind.

He had been talking to Hannah a lot about him, which had helped. Just simple stories about the two of them growing up, nothing serious, but she listened intently like he was reading from the next great American novel. She peppered him with questions, encouraging him to keep going, and Xavier found himself chuckling fondly at some of the memories he hadn't touched in years.

"Nothing out of place turned up on the initial check run on him when he arrived or else it would have been brought to our attention immediately, and he wouldn't still be here. If he uses a different name than Jed Black, though, then we have no way of knowing."

"Since he seems legit on paper, what do you think we should do?" Aaron asked.

"I guess we keep an eye on him," he replied. "Make sure he's not up to something that we've been missing."

Xavier and Aaron turned their attention back to the tub and worked for the better part of another hour before Xavier checked his watch.

"I should go get cleaned up before my meeting with Sarah," he remarked. "Can I leave the rest with you for now?"

"Sure, I'll take it from here," Aaron agreed. "But if this ends up a hot tub by accident, then it's on you."

Xavier grinned. "I have faith in you," he assured him.

Aaron paused for a moment, as if considering his next words. "Everything going okay with Sarah?" he asked.

Xavier shrugged. "Guess so."

"You seem better," Aaron replied.

Xavier was surprised to hear that. He didn't think it would show that quickly, at least not to anyone outside of Hannah. "I do feel better," he admitted. Damn, he meant it, too—that was a new one for him. He had been doing such a good job covering up his real emotions for so long, he had almost forgotten what it felt like to be honest about them. He should have started working with Sarah a long time ago, but at least he was doing it now.

"And how are things going with Hannah?" Aaron asked.

Xavier chuckled. "Hey, at least let me keep some things to myself," he protested, holding his hands up.

"We've all seen you coming out of her cabin every day this week," Aaron pointed out. "If you want to keep it a secret, you're not doing a very good job at it."

"Point taken," Xavier replied with a grin. With that, he said his farewells to Aaron and headed back up to his room.

He supposed he would have to talk to Lawson about

what was going on between him and Hannah. He'd been putting off the conversation because of how angry Lawson had gotten when he learned about Xavier kissing his sister last year. But knowing Hannah left the lodge with him the night of the crash, Lawson had to know they were together.

He wasn't exactly sure what he would call their relationship, being so new, but he loved it. He loved coming back to her cabin every single night, spending an evening with her talking and laughing and…well, the rest of it, too.

He had waited so long to be with her, and now that he was finally getting to enjoy that closeness, he would do anything he could to preserve it. Including taking her seriously with what she had said about Jed, even if he wasn't sure he saw much of it himself.

But he knew Hannah wasn't the kind of person to just start pointing fingers for no reason. She had worked with plenty of people like Jed over the time she had been at the sanctuary. So if she had doubts about his true intentions, he believed that they came from a place of real discomfort. He would need to talk to her a little more about it this evening, reassure her that he and the other guys were looking into the situation.

It was a warm day, now that spring was starting to come around, and he'd ended up pretty sweaty after all the work he'd been doing. He didn't want to subject Sarah to that and he had some time before his appointment, so he headed up to his room to grab a change of clothes to wear after he showered.

But when he reached his door—the door he knew he had locked, just like he always did—he found it pushed open a few inches. Again.

# Chapter Eighteen

"Do I really have to spend the whole afternoon in the office?" Lawson complained as he pulled the door shut behind him. "When we're just getting the first sunshine of the season."

"Yes, you do." Hannah laughed at her brother, pointing firmly to his chair behind the desk. "Go on. Sit down. I want to talk about the finances."

"Good news, right?" he asked her a bit nervously.

"Yeah, great news actually," she assured him with a nod. She had been taking care of the finances at Warrior Peak Sanctuary since they opened. She had never imagined she would be any good at it, but there was something oddly satisfying to her about crunching the numbers, seeing how everything came together and what all was impacted with the changes they implemented. Watching as the sanctuary started to really thrive.

She was sure they would need to hire a full-time accountant eventually, the bigger they got and more money they brought in, but for now, she seemed to be doing a decent job keeping on top of it all. The bills were getting paid and employees got their salaries and their guests were being taken care of in a way that helped them recover and reacclimate to their lives in positive ways. Those were the most important things right now.

"Good," he replied, sitting down in his desk chair and grinning. "Thank God I have you around. I don't know what I would do if you weren't here to keep on top of the practical stuff."

"Yeah, you're lucky," she teased and pulled out the papers she had been working on earlier in the day. She had just finished looking at the intakes and outgoings for the previous year, and it seemed like they were doing exceptionally well.

Along with the funds they received from grants, they worked with several non-profits to raise funds for the upkeep of Warrior Peak. Since the place was originally Xavier's family home, he'd used the family money he'd inherited along with money he and Lawson had scraped together to get them started. Over the past few years, they'd continued to grow from word of mouth and additional donations from previous clients after their time at the lodge.

Lawson and Xavier had also agreed to rent out spaces in the paddocks at some clients' requests, so those who had horses of their own could bring them and tend to them while they stayed at the sanctuary. It became an additional layer of therapy to some, to bring something familiar that they loved and cared for to help ground them. Even Sarah thought it was a great idea, and it had worked out well so far.

"This is the first year we've had enough left over to start thinking about building another expansion," Hannah explained, placing the papers on the desk in front of her brother and running her finger along the numbers to show him just how well they were doing. "I was thinking maybe a separate office for Sarah next to the main lodge here, so she and her clients would have more privacy."

Hannah paused and searched Lawson's face for his immediate reaction to her idea. She didn't usually give specific input to new additions; that was his and Xavier's territory. But she just knew this was a good idea. It would be good for all the people who made appointments with Sarah, especially if they were reluctant to do so, wondering what others thought seeing them visiting her office space at the lodge.

"I've been doing some research and thought the empty section of land right next to the lodge would be perfect. It would be more secluded and quieter for her patients than having to deal with all the extra noises in the hallway and at the front desk when new people arrive. They'd have more privacy to focus on their needs and recovery. We could even add a connecting hallway between the spaces so clients didn't have to go outside in bad weather."

"I think that sounds like a great idea, Hannah," Lawson agreed, peering down at the numbers and squinting slightly. "How much do you think it'll cost?"

"We'd need to reach out to local contractors and get some estimates to get a better idea of that," she explained. "But I think we could easily cover it with the amount of profit that's come in these last few months especially. And maybe even see what additional funds would be necessary if we wanted to do a whole therapy space down the road, hire more therapists."

Lawson leaned back in his seat, nodding as he listened to her. For some reason, she always found herself a little nervous when she came to her brother with ideas like this. She figured it was a result of him being the older one in the family, the one she turned to for guidance. He had always been around to make the big decisions and put plans in motion.

"You want me to start sending out some feelers?" he asked.

"If you've got the time, that'd be great. If not, if you'll write me out a list of specifics I should inquire about, I don't mind doing it," she offered.

Ever since she and Xavier had started seeing each other properly, she had felt beyond nervous about how her brother was going to react. She was sure he knew about it by now, given that the others seemed to have figured it out, but that didn't mean she wasn't still worried about what he was going to say. In fact, she had called him in to talk finances in the hopes she could get him alone long enough to speak about what was going on with Xavier.

"You trying to get on my good side?" he asked bluntly, always able to see right through her.

She sat back in her chair and clasped her hands in front of her, feeling a buzz of anxiousness in her chest. "Uh, there was something else I wanted to talk to you about," she admitted.

He grinned. That annoying, knowing, brotherly grin that told her he had already guessed where she was going to take this conversation. "Let me take a wild guess," he remarked. "You want to talk about Xavier?"

There it was. She nodded, trying to keep her gaze steady. He didn't seem as angry as he had before, but did he know the extent of their involvement? Was he trying to look the other way? How would he respond when he found out that they had basically been living together since the accident the week before last? "Yes, it's about Xavier," she confessed, her voice wavering slightly as she spoke.

She could still remember the look of thunderous anger on Lawson's face when he had found out last time about them kissing. As upset as he was then, it was hard to believe he would just suddenly let it go. Of course, she hoped his feelings had changed and things were different this time, but she wouldn't know for sure until she brought it up.

However, no matter what he said, it wasn't going to change her mind about pursuing a relationship with Xavier now. She wasn't going to let her brother dictate how she lived her life, no matter how angry he was about what she was doing. She was falling for Xavier, hard and fast, and she wasn't going to let a damn thing get in the way of that.

"I know that my interest in Xavier has caused issues in the past," she explained, not taking her eyes from his face as she spoke, watching every little reaction, every shift in his expression. "And I know that you're just being protective of me. But I... The two of us are together now. Really together. We've had feelings for each other for a long time, and I'm not willing to ignore them anymore, and neither is he. And neither of us want this to get in the way of our relationships with you. I want your blessing for this, as my brother. If you'll give it to me."

He paused for an excruciating second before he responded. A smile spread wide across his face. "Of course you have my blessing, Hannah."

Her eyes widened. "But I thought... I mean, the way you reacted before—"

"I wasn't thinking straight back then, and I'm sorry

about that," he admitted. "We should have spoken about this way before now," Lawson rose from behind the desk and rounded it to stand in front of his sister. He folded his arms across his chest and leaned back against the desk. "I saw how much Xavier was struggling after he'd lost his brother, and all I could think about was you being the front line to have to deal with that. You're my baby sister, and I was concerned about what might happen, how it would affect you."

Hannah reached out and squeezed his forearm.

"I care about you both so much, and I want you both to be happy, but I just couldn't see how he could be with anyone without pulling them into all his struggles. I didn't think witnessing all that would be good for you." Lawson swallowed heavily, and she could tell how hard it was for him to even talk about his best friend like that.

But Lawson had been there with Xavier from the start. From the moment he had arrived home, when he had been forced to deal with the loss of his brother while also dealing with his parents blaming him and, as a result, having no one to stand by his side and help him through his grief.

Hannah knew Lawson had done his best to be there for Xavier, but what Xavier had really needed was the support and care of his family since they were all dealing with the same grief and loss. Her brother had seen how much he struggled, and it was no wonder he had been so protective about letting his little sister get too close.

"He's been working with Sarah, and he's doing so much better now," she assured him. "It's amazing how far he's come. He's actually started talking about Max to me for the first time."

Lawson's face lit up. "Really?" he replied in amazement. "Damn, I never thought we'd get to that point. That's wonderful."

"I know," she murmured, and she felt a swell of pride when she thought of how well Xavier was doing. And he was only just getting started, there was still so much room for him to grow. Hannah wanted nothing more than to see him come out the other side of it a better, stronger man. A man who didn't blame himself for what had happened, finally free of the guilt he had carried for so long.

"I've been trying to convince him to talk to Sarah about all of this for so long," Lawson remarked, shaking his head. "I didn't think he was ever going to actually do it, but you must have changed his mind. You must have given him a reason."

She lowered her gaze, smiling at the thought. The fact Xavier was willing to put himself through something as tough and demanding as therapy now that they were together meant the world to her. It felt like an investment in their future as a couple, his intentions clear—he wanted to make sure she got the best version of him, and he was putting in the effort to bring that version to life.

"So, you're really okay with us?" she asked her brother, shifting in her seat.

"Hannah, I just want you to be safe and happy. If being with Xavier is what you really want and you have no doubts about being with him while he deals with his trauma, then I will not stand in your way," he replied sincerely. "Hey, it's going to keep my Christmas card list short, right?"

She couldn't help but burst out laughing at that part. That was so typical of Lawson to turn all of this tension and stress that had hung in the air between them into a joke. "Yeah, guess so," she agreed, and she stood up to give him a hug. "It really means a lot to me, you know that, right? I wouldn't want to be with him if I thought it was going to be a problem for you."

"I know," he replied and pulled her close. "And I appreciate that. I'm sorry for trying to get in the way of it before, but I've learned my lesson. I can see how good the two of you are together. I'm not going to cause any trouble, I promise."

"Thank you," she murmured into his shoulder. "And please don't start pulling out my baby photos and telling him embarrassing childhood stories about me, okay?"

"Hey, it's my job!" he protested and pulled back with a laugh. "I'm your big brother. If I don't embarrass you in front of your new boyfriend, who will?"

She giggled, but at the back of her mind, she felt a warmth tingling through her at the sound of that word. *Boyfriend.* She and Xavier hadn't put a label on their relationship yet, but she liked the way it sounded, liked the way it felt. She could definitely get used to that label.

For so long, she had been alone. She had watched the women around her get close to men, fall in love, develop partnerships that would last a lifetime. She was happy for her friends but terribly envious at the same time. She never thought she'd have that kind of happiness for herself. Now, she got to include Xavier and herself into that equation.

"I should get going," she told her brother, stepping toward the office door. "Can you talk to Xavier about this, too? Make sure he knows you're okay with it?"

He nodded. "Of course I will." Then, as she opened the

door and walked into the hall, he called after her, "And I'll make sure to tell him what a brat you are!"

"Don't you dare!" she yelled back over her shoulder, but she was already laughing. This was the last detail she needed to fall into place to feel totally confident about moving forward with Xavier.

She felt like a huge weight had been lifted. They didn't have to worry about hiding anything from anyone. They were free to be open about their relationship to everyone and finally be happy together.

Her feet felt as though they barely touched the floor as she skipped off down the corridor, a grin so wide on her face it felt as though it might burst. She knew Lawson was going to speak to Xavier, but she couldn't wait to celebrate the good news. He was already taking steps to heal himself, working on his mental health and coming to terms with his past. This would be another good step forward.

## Chapter Nineteen

Xavier cautiously pushed his bedroom door open and stepped inside, looking for anything that seemed out of place. And damn, there was a whole lot in here that didn't look right.

His eyes widened as he took it all in. The covers had been tossed back off his bed, the pillows slashed—even the mattress had been pulled up at the sides, as though someone had been searching underneath it. The dresser drawers had been opened and rummaged through, some of them having fallen out in the search. The window was pushed open, and the screen had been knocked out.

His shower and his appointment with Sarah were forgotten; he needed to find out who had done this and just what they had been looking for.

A sudden thought occurred… Were they still here?

He couldn't sense anyone in the room with him, but they might be hiding. He opened the closet cautiously and then checked under the bed, but it seemed like it was just him.

His mind raced. What did they want? Did they find whatever it was? He couldn't see anything that had been taken, at least not right away, but his room was such a mess that it was impossible to tell. He would need to sift through the piles of his stuff before he would know for sure.

Xavier knew he needed to think clearly and not let panic get the better of him. He drew in a few long breaths, trying to remember all the tools Sarah had given him to navigate his emotions, but it wasn't working. He started to shut down; his mind felt far away from his body.

What could they have possibly been looking for? As he stood there, rolling the question around in his head, something finally struck him.

If he was right about this…then he was in bigger trouble than he thought. He needed a weapon, fast.

The safe in the back of his closet had a gun. He'd stored one there months ago but hoped he would never have to use. Now he was glad it was there because he needed it for whatever came next. He had to be armed if he was going to take on whoever had come in here. This was the second time his room had been searched and from the destruction this time, they were escalating.

He dropped to his knees in his closet, shifting stuff around and reaching toward the back for the gun safe when he felt a crack on the back of his skull.

He pitched forward with a groan.

*Damn!* Whoever had come to his room wasn't done with him yet. He should have called for backup as soon as he noticed his door ajar instead of trying to do it alone, but he didn't feel as though he had a choice. He had to move fast.

He tried to push himself up and turn to face his attacker, but before he was able, he felt the pressure of a cord around his neck. Someone jerked him backward out of the closet and into his room. He started to panic, but then his instincts and training kicked in.

He pushed a hand between his neck and the cord around his throat, creating just enough leverage for him to move his head forward and keep the cord from doing its job.

Whoever was behind him moved in closer to try to get better leverage on his neck. As soon as he was sure they were in range, Xavier slammed his head back, landing a blow against their nose that made a sickening crunch.

The cord loosened for a moment, and Xavier ducked out of it, sliding to one side and panting for breath. His adrenaline was pumping, bringing him back to all the worst times of his life, but he couldn't let those memories get to him now. Whoever was attacking him was out for blood—he was going to have to fight them in order to stay alive.

He managed to spin around, but his eyes were still blurry from the blow he'd just taken. Still, he could make out a man standing above him. The mask he was wearing hid the man's identity, but he was tall, muscular, and had hatred burning in his eyes. The man muttered a curse, wiping his nose as blood dripped down the mask and into his mouth. His hand was left with a dark red streak from where he had swiped it across his face smearing the blood. He flashed Xavier an eerie smile.

And something about that smile made Xavier's blood run cold. He knew that kind of smile. It was the smile of a sadistic person who would kill or seriously injure someone without a second thought.

The man lifted the baton he was holding above his

head and brought it down, the sound of it cutting through the air.

Xavier managed to roll out of the way just in time, and it slammed into the wall next to him. He was breathing hard, trying to pull himself together. He thought about calling out for help, but this part of the building would be deserted by now. Nobody would hear him, and he would have lost vital time trying to get aid when he knew he had to do this himself.

"Come on, Dutch," the man taunted.

Dutch? Xavier stilled, muscles going taut as his vision began to clear. That name. He hadn't heard that name in years.

The man standing above him suddenly took a step back and ripped off the mask.

Jed. All the pieces suddenly clicked into place: Hannah and Aaron's concerns, the feeling like he'd seen the man somewhere before, the car crash and generators...

There was only one person who had ever called Xavier by that name.

"How do you know that name?" Xavier asked as he tried to pull himself to his feet. His head was killing him. He reached around to touch the spot where the baton had hit him, and he felt the hot rush of blood beneath his fingers. Looked like he wasn't the only one who had managed to get in a good blow.

"Learned it from a colleague of mine. Does the name Sampson ring any bells? From what he told me, I thought you'd put up more of a fight." A smile tugged at the corners of Jed's bloodied mouth.

Xavier clenched his fists at his sides, trying to get his anger under control. It had been so many years since he'd heard Sampson's name, and he couldn't believe he was hearing it now. The one man he had hoped he would never run into again. "Just go," Xavier told him, voice low. "Nobody has to know you were ever here or that you're working with Sampson. Just get out of here. You hear me?"

Jed chuckled, twirling the baton in his hand as he took a step closer.

Xavier's eyes darted to the door, hoping no one else was going to walk in and get hurt. What if Sarah showed up looking for him, or worse yet, Hannah?

No, he had to stop this now. It was up to him to get Jed out of here before something worse happened. Even though his vision was blurry and his skull felt like it would split open at any moment, he had to fight back.

Jed had infiltrated the sanctuary with one purpose— to find out about Xavier. His weaknesses and vulnerabilities. This man had known just where to strike him to make his mark, too. His experience was evident. He knew what he was doing.

And Xavier was a little out of practice. Not the best time to realize it, but he still had some fight in him. Especially when it came to protecting this place and his friends.

"All you have to do is tell me where it is," Jed growled, his voice low and threatening. "And then, I'll walk away from here. You'll never have to deal with me or Sampson ever again. Isn't that what you want?"

Xavier wished he could believe him. Hell, if he thought it would work like that, he would have handed it over a long time ago, but he knew it didn't. He knew Sampson would never stop. He would never back off, never stop coming after him. He wouldn't quit until he had what he wanted—and until he made Xavier pay for keeping it from him, too.

"I don't know what you're talking about," Xavier spat back at him.

A lie, and they both knew it. All the questions Xavier had asked himself about what was going on here and why it was happening were becoming clear. He was a target again, because of his past. Because of something he thought was over long ago.

But he should have known by now that his nightmares didn't have a habit of going down without a fight. He had to take them on himself—and if that meant fighting back again, he would do it.

Jed shook his head, letting out a long, demonstrative sigh. "I was hoping you would play along," he remarked.

Xavier leaned heavily against the dresser trying to steady himself. His head was spinning, and he was having a hard time keeping himself upright. The blow Jed had landed at the back of his head had been carefully crafted to render him helpless, a practiced move to immediately weaken his opponent. It was working, too. Xavier felt almost as weak as a newborn kitten. The other man had the perfect opportunity to take him out in his current state.

Jed quickly lifted the baton again and bought it down with a sharp strike on to Xavier's shoulder. Xavier let out a gritted cry of pain, trying to swerve out of the way of the next one, but the other man was too quick—or Xavier was too slow—following with another strike to his other arm.

Excruciating pain radiated through Xavier's entire system; he wasn't used to taking this type of beating anymore. It had been so long since he had been in the midst of an active fight, and he was rusty.

Jed swept his legs out from under him, and Xavier managed to catch himself before he landed face-first on the floor. This man knew exactly how to disable someone and make it impossible for them to fight back. More than that, he realized, Jed had been shown the exact moves Xavier had been taught in his own training.

He wasn't sure why he was just now realizing that fact, but Jed must have been trained by the CIA, just like he was. He knew the tricks of the trade, just like Xavier. How to expose and exploit weaknesses and then go in for the kill.

And he was willing to do whatever it took to get what he wanted from Xavier, use any opportunity to his advantage to win. He took a step forward, crushing one of Xavier's hands under his leather boot.

Xavier groaned in agony, ripping his hand back before his fingers snapped beneath the pressure. His whole body was consumed with fiery pain all at once, and he tried to pull himself upright again, but it was too late. Xavier had nothing left.

Jed stood above him, baton in one hand, bloodstained smile painted on his face. As he lifted the baton above his head once more, Xavier closed his eyes and braced himself for the next blow.

# Chapter Twenty

Feeling as though she could walk on air, Hannah made her way down to Sarah's office with a grin. She was planning to talk to Sarah about the new addition they wanted to add to the lodge to be able to provide more people with the therapy they needed. If there was anyone who would have some good ideas for how to best expand their therapy department, it would her.

And maybe Hannah wanted to share a little of her excitement with Sarah, too. She was so pleased that her brother had finally given his blessing for her to pursue a relationship with Xavier like she had wanted to for years.

Now that she'd spoken with her brother, his previous reactions made sense to her. Of course he was worried about her getting involved with Xavier; he was Xavier's best friend and knew that he was dealing with so much. Because he was also Hannah's brother, he wanted to keep her safe and didn't want her to be dragged into Xavier's issues. Anyone would have been protective in a situation like that.

But now, after their chat and knowing the hard work Xavier was putting into therapy to face his nightmares and heal from his trauma, there was no reason for Lawson to try to stop them from being together. He could see how good they were together, how happy they made each other.

Hannah couldn't wait to prove to her brother and everyone else, including herself, that the wait had been worth it now that they were finally together.

She had checked Sarah's therapy schedule, and she didn't have any appointments booked until Xavier's, which wasn't for another forty-five minutes, so she would likely be in her office writing up patient notes or sending emails. She didn't want to interrupt Sarah's quiet work time, but she knew that her friend would want to know the good news since she had suspected that something was going on between Hannah and Xavier for a long time.

Hardly able to contain her excitement, Hannah lifted her hand and rapped on the door. She listened for a moment, but there was no reply. She frowned and knocked again, but there was still nothing. Maybe she'd had a last-minute request for an emergency appointment. Sometimes, with the problems they were dealing with, the guests in residence needed access to immediate care. Sarah always obliged, as long as it didn't interfere with another patient who needed her.

Hannah was about to chalk it up to that and try back later when a thought struck her. Normally, if she was with a patient, Sarah would have just called through the door to tell her that she'd be out in an hour or so. The silence wasn't like her.

Hannah turned back to the door again, staring at it, suddenly feeling uneasiness rising up in her chest. She knocked again, a little louder this time, just in case Sarah was listening to music through headphones or something, but there was still no reply. Pressing her ear to the door, she couldn't hear anything. She was pretty sure the office was empty. Which meant it wouldn't be a big deal at all if she just pushed the door open and checked to make sure everything was okay.

She should just leave it alone, but her instincts were telling her that something was wrong and she needed to check it out. She tried the handle, and it was unlocked. When she pushed the door open and stepped through, she gasped at what she saw.

The office was completely and utterly trashed. Paintings hung askew on the walls, one of the chairs had been ripped open, and white stuffing overflowed like a twisted version of a snowscape. Pens were scattered all over the floor, and papers had been knocked to the ground. The desk drawers were torn open where someone had clearly been searching through them and the computer that usually sat on the desk was upside down next to it.

"Oh my God," Hannah gasped out loud, a cold grip of terror taking hold of her. Her eyes darted around the room as she tried to make sense of what she was seeing. Who would have done this? One of the clients could have just freaked out and gone on a destruction spree, but that didn't sound or feel right. This seemed deliberate, like a weird sort of organized chaos.

Someone was looking for something. But what? And why here in Sarah's office? And where was Sarah?

Hannah was just about to turn around and go in search of Xavier or Lawson for help, when she heard a noise.

"Hannah?" a tiny voice squeaked from underneath the desk.

Hannah dropped to her knees to look underneath it.

Sarah looked back at her, wide-eyed, trembling and clutching her knees to her chest.

"Sarah, what happened?" Hannah gaped at her. "Are you okay?"

"I'm... I'm okay," Sarah replied, her voice shaky.

Hannah rushed around the desk and offered her a hand to help her to her feet.

Sarah took it gratefully, grabbing on to the side of the desk for support as she tried to gather herself.

"You need something to drink? Do you need me to call River to check you over?" Hannah fussed over her urgently.

Sarah shook her head. "No, nothing like that," she replied. "I—I'm okay. Physically, I mean. I just..." She cast her gaze around the office, taking in the extent of the damage for what seemed to be the first time. She pressed her lips together, the distress written all over her face. "I..." she began, but then, the tears fell down her cheeks, the shock clearly getting to her.

Hannah had never seen her so shaken up before and instantly pulled Sarah into a protective hug, hating that she had been through something so scary.

Once Sarah managed to catch her breath again, Hannah pulled back slightly and raised her eyebrows. "What happened here?" she asked gently. She knew it was going to be hard for Sarah to talk about, but if the person who had done this was still loose in the building or on the property, it was important they figured it out before something else happened.

"Jed," Sarah finally breathed.

Hannah's heart dropped slightly. She knew there was something off with that guy. "What did he do?" she asked.

Sarah shook her head, clearly having a hard time going through the details again, even in her head. "He…he came in here for an appointment," she explained. "And I thought everything was normal. But he walked in, and as soon as the door was shut, he locked it, and he just started trashing my office. Started going through my files, going through the desk, the computer, everything. He told me that if Xavier didn't have it, then it had to be in here."

"It?" Hannah replied.

"Your guess is as good as mine," Sarah admitted with a shrug. "I have no idea what he meant. There's nothing in here worth taking." She trembled hard as she looked back up at Hannah. "I think Xavier might be in danger."

Now the break-in to Xavier's room made sense. Jed was searching for whatever he thought Xavier had in his room. Was that why Hannah had gotten such weird vibes from him right from the beginning? Why others had seen him lurking around? Had he just turned up here because he thought Xavier had something he wanted?

Hannah tried to remember what Xavier was supposed to be doing right then. He had been with Aaron, right? And then he was supposed to have an appointment with Sarah. She needed to go find him. Now. Tell him she was right about Jed and he was the one who had been in his room and about him trashing Sarah's office because he was searching for something he thought Xavier had.

None of this made sense to her, but hopefully Xavier would be able to make sense of it all. First, she had to find him.

"You call Lawson," Hannah instructed Sarah, pulling herself together. "Tell him what Jed did and that he's looking for something but we don't know what. And then call Bailey and tell her what happened. She'll send people up or she'll come herself. I've got to find Xavier and tell him what's going on."

"You sure?" Sarah asked. "Jed could be somewhere close watching and waiting to see what we'll do. He could even be listening in right now."

"After this," Hannah replied, looking around the room at all the destruction. "I doubt he's still around since he didn't find what he was looking for. Plus, he's got to know that you'll report him. But we can't wait around either way. The guys need to know what's going on and everyone needs to be on the lookout now."

"How can we be sure that it's just him?" Sarah replied nervously.

Hannah frowned. "Did he say anything that might make you think otherwise?" she asked, her heart sinking. How many of them were there around here? How many of these guys had managed to infiltrate the sanctuary? She mentally flicked through all the people she had registered at the lodge in the last few weeks, trying to remember if any of them had given her a strange feeling the same way Jed had, but she couldn't think of anyone else. She would need to go through the files, see if there was anything suspicious in there.

But right now, there was a more pressing matter on her mind. She needed to get to Xavier and tell him Jed was searching for him and whatever he thought Xavier had. She wasn't going to stand by and let the man she loved get hurt or walk into a trap unawares.

Sarah wrapped her arms around her wait. "No, he didn't mention anyone else. That doesn't mean someone else isn't around watching or waiting. Just be careful, Hannah."

Hannah nodded and threw open the office door before she lost her nerve. Before she could race off down the corridor, a man stepped in front of her, leveling a gun at her head.

Her feet froze to the spot. She had never been on the other end of a gun and had no idea how to react. It was like her breath had seized in her chest, and she couldn't find her voice. She wanted to cry out, but all she could do was stare down the dark, dangerous barrel of the weapon pointed in her face.

And at the man on the other side of it.

*Jed.*

His nose was bloody and swollen, and his lips were stained with the same redness. But there was a maniacal grin on his face, as though he didn't even notice his injury. The look in his eyes scared her almost as much as the gun he had pointed at her.

He slowly turned the gun to Sarah. "Put that phone down," he ordered.

Hannah's head was spinning. What the hell was going on? Why was Jed back, here of all places? Why didn't he leave when he couldn't find whatever he was searching for?

Hannah turned to Sarah, nodding at her to do as he said. They could work this out, as long as neither of them ended up with a bullet in their brain. Sarah slowly placed the phone back down on the desk, her hand visibly shaking, her face white. Hannah wished she could comfort her, but right now, she had to focus on getting them out of there alive. She couldn't let her panic get the better of her, no matter how terrifying the situation was.

"Good girl," Jed sneered, patronizing as always.

Hannah felt a flare of anger at his remark. But how he spoke to them was the least of her concerns right now. She needed to make sure she got both of them out of this mess without getting hurt. She would never be able to forgive herself if Sarah got injured because of her rashness.

"You, come with me," Jed ordered Hannah, jerking the gun toward her.

Hannah stood her ground. "Where are you taking me?"

"That is no concern of yours," he replied, flashing her a grin. "You just shut that pretty face and do as I say, you understand? Or someone's going to get hurt."

Fear rippled through Hannah at his demand. She wished she had a way to get by him without getting shot and find help. Even if she could get out in the hallway and yell at the top of her lungs it would be better than doing nothing. There were always people around this side of the lodge; someone would hear. But then they'd be put in harm's way because of her, and Hannah couldn't have that on her conscience.

She couldn't believe this was happening again. More danger to the lodge and its guests. First the fire several months ago, and now this. This was supposed to be a safe place, where people could forget their worries and concentrate on healing and bettering themselves. Instead, it seemed to have turned into a place where danger followed and threatened their family and friends. Hannah wanted to jump on Jed and claw his eyes out for the evil and terror he'd brought to their peaceful doorstep.

But she pushed down her violent urge with a calming breath. "Fine. I'll go with you," she murmured. "Just leave Sarah and the others alone."

"You don't have a choice, bitch." He laughed and pushed the tip of the gun right up to her forehead."

Hannah's lungs seized, and she started shaking. She couldn't help it. She didn't want to die here, not like this.

"Hannah—" Sarah attempted, but Jed turned the gun on her again, silencing her once more.

"I'm not letting a pair of bitches stand in the way of millions of dollars," he told them. "Move, Hannah. Now." He reached out and yanked her forward so fast she crashed into his chest.

She pushed back and tried to move away, but Jed pulled her back to him as he stalked out the door with her in tow.

As soon as they cleared the doorway, he grabbed her shoulder and shoved the gun in the small of her back, pushing her down the corridor. He was moving her at a rate faster than her feet could keep up, and she stumbled several times. As soon as she'd right herself, Jed would jam the gun in her spine again and keep shoving her forward.

She knew she needed to fight back, do something to try to get away, but with him constantly forcing the gun to her back, she couldn't think straight. She wasn't sure what she could do without getting her brains blown out.

Closing her eyes, she kept walking, counting her footsteps and praying that Xavier would somehow know where to find her. She wasn't sure exactly how that was going to happen, but she had faith in him.

And faith in him seemed like the only thing she could hold on to right now without losing her mind entirely.

# Chapter Twenty-One

"Xavier, can you hear me?"

Xavier's eyes flickered open. What? Where was he again? He couldn't even remember. All he could think about was the pulsing, throbbing pain at the back of his head and the blurriness of his vision. He felt hands on his shoulders, someone trying to shake him awake, and he managed to focus his gaze on the person in front of him.

"Aaron?" he mumbled. "Don't do that, man." The shaking was making him nauseous.

"Yeah, it's me, Aaron," the man replied, sounding relieved. "Can you see me okay? Can you hear me?"

"You're a little fuzzy, but yeah, I think so," Xavier replied, trying to sit up. He winced as a jolt of pain rushed through his system again. He sank back down, letting out a groan as the memories began to surface.

"Do you know where you're bleeding from?" Aaron asked.

"My head," Xavier mumbled. "The back of my head, I think." He tried to reach up to touch it, but Aaron caught his hand.

"Let's not do that, all right? We'll get it looked over," Aaron promised. "Come on, let's see if we can get you up."

He managed to lift Xavier off the ground and get him

planted on the edge of his bed, the mattress barely still on the frame. Everything was spinning.

Aaron sat beside him to get a look at his wound just as Lawson appeared in the doorway to his room.

"What the hell is going on?" Lawson demanded.

"Your guess is as good as mine," Aaron replied. "I heard a commotion in here, and when I came in, Xavier was down for the count but no one else was around. That's when I called you."

"Damn," Lawson muttered, shooting a look of concern at Xavier. But more than anything, Xavier could see the anger in his eyes. He knew that was how Lawson dealt with shock, but right now, he needed his best friend on his side.

"Do you know who attacked you?" Lawson demanded.

"Jed," Xavier replied, wincing as Aaron poked around at the back of his skull.

"Jed?" Lawson sounded surprised. "What happened?"

"I came to grab a change of clothes for the shower and the door was open again. I noticed the room trashed and was going to grab my gun and he nailed me from behind. We fought some and he got in a final hit and took off."

Lawson frowned in confusion. "Why would he attack you and trash your room? That doesn't make sense."

Xavier closed his eyes, trying to fight the nausea rolling up his throat. "Jed's looking for something he thought I had." He paused and sighed. "It's complicated." He chanced a quick look at Aaron, then locked his eyes on Lawson.

"He's not working alone," Xavier replied, starting to shake his head, then thought better of it. The movement was making his eyesight worse. "He called me something—a name I haven't heard since my CIA days. I'm certain he's working with someone I used to know. Someone called… Sampson."

Saying the name out loud seemed like a bad omen. But he knew he had to. He had tried to leave that part of his life behind, but clearly, he wasn't going to be able to get away quite so easily.

"Sampson?" Lawson asked, frowning. "You never mentioned anything about a Sampson before. And I don't remember meeting anyone by that name at the agency."

"He was another operative I worked with when we were on separate squads at the agency," Xavier explained. "The two of us had a few difficult missions together. I always got a strange vibe from him, but he never really did anything that gave me a concrete reason for that. It was just more of an unease of how he carried himself and certain things he said, so I just pushed it to the back of my mind and kept doing my job. Figured that was the best thing for me to do. Not make extra waves and complicate things further."

"But?" Lawson prompted him.

"The last mission we were on, it went sideways," Xavier explained with a sigh. He hadn't thought about this in so long. He had hoped he wouldn't have to deal with it ever again. He'd tried so hard to leave it in the past.

"In what way?" Aaron asked him.

Xavier reached to the back of his head, brushing his fingers against the bloody gash in his skull. He winced. He was going to need to be stitched up and checked for a concussion sooner or later, but right now, they had to deal with the issue at hand. "We were assigned to this case, tracking a lost arms shipment that we had reason to believe was going to fall into the wrong hands," he explained. "But the more time I spent on the case, the more obvious it became to me that Sampson *was* the wrong hands. He dropped a few hints about the two of us working together, coming up with a cover story so we could sell them ourselves."

"So what exactly are they looking for here?" Lawson asked. "What do they think you have?"

"A USB drive." Xavier sighed. "It was the one with all the information about the shipment, all the tracking details we had on it. I was supposed to pass it on to Sampson so we could find the container, but I destroyed it before he could get his hands on it. I knew I couldn't risk firepower like that ending up in rotation with the wrong kind of people. It was a tough choice, but I know it was the right one."

"But he doesn't know you've destroyed it," Aaron surmised. "And he sent someone to infiltrate the lodge to try to find out where you were keeping it."

"That's what I think," Xavier agreed.

"You think he would kill to get his hands on it?" Lawson's voice hardened.

"Definitely. He's killed before," Xavier replied, with a grimace. "When we were working together, he was always trigger-happy. Most of the time, they were the kind of people who would have ended up dead one way or another because of their line of work. Sampson just took great pleasure in being the one who pulled the trigger."

"Why do you think he's come after you now?" Aaron wondered out loud.

Xavier sighed again. "I don't know," he admitted. "I guess because he finally tracked me down and found a way to get closer to me without arousing any suspicion. Sending Jed in first… I don't know what he's promised that guy, but I think he'll just take him out the first chance he gets. He uses people to get what he wants. And he's going to use whatever means he can to get his hands on that USB drive."

"That doesn't even exist anymore," Lawson finished up for him. "Do you think he's going to believe it when you try to tell him that?"

"No," Xavier replied. "From what I know about this guy, he's going to put up as much of a fight as he can. That's definitely what Jed was looking for in here."

"And where did he go?" Lawson asked urgently. "Do you have any idea where he is now?"

Xavier slowly shook his head. "I wish I did, but he knocked me out and then took off. Next thing I knew, Aaron was waking me up here."

"Hell," Lawson muttered and began pacing back and forth.

Xavier could practically see his mind racing. His own was going a hundred miles an hour, despite the aching pain at the back of his head. He couldn't think straight. Was Sampson here on the grounds? Had he been watching from afar, making sure that his plan came together? Though he might have been a psycho, he wasn't stupid— he wouldn't have made it that far in the CIA if he was. Jed had to be in contact with him somehow to get his orders. Now they just needed to find Jed.

*Hannah.* Xavier felt a flood of terror grip him when he thought of her. She was out there, and she didn't know what had just happened. Yes, she had her doubts about Jed, but she wasn't aware of just how serious things had gotten. Hopefully, if she saw him, she would know to steer clear of him, but Xavier needed to get to her and catch her up on everything that had gone down. He would never forgive himself if something happened to her and he hadn't been there to stop it.

"I'll call Bailey, tell her to come up here and get a statement from you and process the crime scene," Aaron offered. "And I'll ask her to bring River along to look at that wound on your head and check for a concussion." He stepped out into the hallway, phone in hand.

"I need to get to Hannah," Xavier growled, trying to get to his feet.

Lawson put a hand on his shoulder and pushed him back down again. "You need to sit your ass right there and wait to get checked over," he replied firmly.

Xavier knew there would be no arguing with him.

"You can't walk into a fight with a wound like that on your head. You're going to be more of a liability than anything else," Lawson pointed out in his infuriatingly calm and logical way. "Now, tell me everything you remember about Sampson. He might have other people here he's been using to watch you. We've had an influx of new guests this week alone."

Xavier tried to catch Lawson up on every detail he remembered, but they were hazy. Their time at the CIA was long behind them—or so he'd thought. It had been the incident with Sampson that had driven him to leave in the first place, because he knew he couldn't handle winding up on a mission with someone else like him again.

He needed to get out and do things on his own terms, and he couldn't rely on the CIA to do the right thing. There were plenty of agents who had to be aware of what

Sampson was up to, but they were willing to look the other way, either because they were scared of him or they were on his side.

And Xavier had no idea if that made him the enemy here. What if Sampson had the full force of the CIA behind him? Xavier would bet money that Jed had been an operative before Sampson pulled him into this, hell, maybe he still was. He seemed to have a certain comfort with putting on an act the way he had since he arrived here, as though it wasn't the first time he had gone undercover.

After Aaron had called Bailey, he stepped back into the room, eyes darting between him and Lawson, his face pale.

Xavier's stomach turned, and his nausea came on full force. He knew before Aaron even opened his mouth something terrible was wrong. There was only one reason he would have that look on his face. Xavier swallowed heavily, trying to prepare himself for the worst.

Lawson sensing the same, clenched his fists at his sides. "What is it? What's wrong?"

"Bailey just got off the phone with Sarah. There'd been an incident in her office, so Bailey's on the way. But…" His gaze shifted between the two men again. "It's Hannah. They've taken her."

"Jed." Xavier all but growled. He closed his eyes and took several deep breaths trying to control the immediate range that flooded his system. Tuning out Lawson's forceful steps pacing the room and his muttered curses.

That was the one thing he didn't want to hear above everything else—the one person he couldn't lose. Not now. Not after they'd just come clean about their feelings for each other and were finally together in the way he'd always hoped for. Hannah had always been special to him, but now she was his to protect. He wouldn't let her slip through his fingers. He wouldn't let some ghost from his past snatch her away.

He didn't care what it took. He was going to get her back. Sampson and Jed didn't know what kind of storm they had coming their way.

# Chapter Twenty-Two

*In, out, in, out, in, out.* Hannah tried to count each breath as it came, doing everything she could to keep the panic from getting the better of her.

But as she sat in the back seat of the black Ford she had been bundled into, her hands bound behind her, she didn't know how much longer she could hold out.

Jed had forced her out the back door of the lodge and into his truck—the same one that had driven them off the road that night, she was sure of it. Wrapping her wrists in a plastic cuff, he had shoved her in the back and told her to keep her mouth shut.

She had done as she was told. She knew better than to fight him on this, when she was so clearly at a disadvantage. She didn't know where he'd taken her, some secluded wooded area, but she knew she just needed to stay alive, and then…

And then what? Then hopefully Lawson and Xavier would find her. She didn't know how, though. They might not even know she was gone yet. Shoving down her panic once more, she peered out through the windshield of the truck where Jed was talking with another man.

Suddenly, Jed stalked over to the vehicle and threw the

door opposite her open, grabbed her arm and yanked her out. "You're coming with me," he snarled.

She stumbled, trying to catch herself as he pulled her toward the side door of a white van sitting just a few feet off the road. She glanced around as she was pulled along but didn't recognize the area. He had taken a road away from the sanctuary she hadn't noticed before. They were parked close to the tree line where they couldn't be immediately seen. She could only guess this other man was his partner in some way.

If that was true, then Xavier was in even more danger since she had only mentioned her concerns to him about Jed. He wasn't aware anyone else was involved and she had no way to warn him.

She took a chance and glanced at the other man as Jed dragged her along.

He didn't even pay attention to her, his eyes only glanced up briefly from the phone he held in front of him, but the sight of him sent a shiver down her spine nonetheless. His hair was shaved close to his head, his eyes dark, almost black. Even from the brief moment he looked at her, she could tell they seemed blank, like those of a shark cutting through the water toward their prey. He wore large combat boots and a flak jacket—dressed, she noted to herself, like someone who was going to complete a messy job.

Was she that job?

Hannah hardly had time to think about it before Jed thrust her into the open door of the van, standing guard just next to her so she didn't think about trying to escape.

That wouldn't stop her though. She had to think of something.

She eyed the gun on his belt, wondering if he would turn it back on her soon. Her eyes darted to the window on the other side of the vehicle, noticing how close the van was to the tree line, but she knew she wouldn't be able to make a run for it with her hands behind her back and Jed standing right there. He'd snatch her back or shoot her before she took a step. No, she realized there was nothing she could do. She just had to sit tight, and…and hope for the best. Even if it killed her to be so passive right now.

She peered out of the van as the other man made a call. He lifted the phone to his ear, a grin spreading over his face but not reaching his eyes.

"Dutch," the man greeted whoever was on the other end of the line. "Long time, no talk. How's your head?"

Hannah strained to try to hear more, but he'd turned his back to the van and he was too far away. She tucked her legs up underneath her, scooting across the floor to lean against the wall of the van. Jed shot her a look, as though warning her not to push her luck, and she met his gaze with a defiance she mustered up from somewhere inside of her.

"Watch it," he hissed at her.

She glowered back at him. From somewhere, she could smell the metallic scent of blood—not hers. She glanced around the van and noticed a large box in the back. Unease rolled through her at the sight of it. She prayed that didn't have something to do with her. Hannah was about to ask what it was when the mystery man turned back around facing her and started talking again. She tuned in to the conversation once more.

"You bring me that drive, or we kill the girl, it's that simple," he explained. "And come alone, Dutch. I don't want to see any of your lodge friends with you. Just you and me, like the old days, right?"

Dutch? Who was Dutch? Hannah racked her brain, trying to remember if she had ever run into someone by that name or anything close to it at Warrior Peak, but she couldn't come up with anything. But she knew one thing for sure—she was *the girl* he was threatening.

She started to feel lightheaded, the shock of all of this settling in. They were threatening to kill her if this Dutch person—whoever they were—didn't give them what they wanted. She was completely and utterly helpless, at the mercy of these evil men, and it scared the hell out of her.

She wasn't used to things being out of her control like this. She was the one who was supposed to decide how her life turned out. But not this time. She was relying on someone she had never even heard of before to give these men what they wanted.

Why would this Dutch person care whether they killed her or not? What if they killed her anyway? From the lengths they'd already gone to in order to find this drive, who was to say they wouldn't destroy the entire lodge and all the guests to not have witnesses when they got what they wanted.

*Oh God...*

Spots started to dance in front of her eyes. She was starting to let the panic consume her, and she was hyperventilating. *Deep breaths. Slow and easy breaths.* She couldn't pass out, not now. But she needed to get farther away, put more space between her and the open door. Make it harder for Jed to get his hands on her again, should he try to yank her out.

The box…

As quietly as possible, Hannah shifted herself around and slowly inched her way to the back of the van where the box sat, taunting her. She needed to know what was in there. Maybe there was something she could use to help her escape. She kept shooting glances at Jed's back to make sure he wasn't aware of her movements. He truly scared her, and she didn't want his full wrath turned against her. The look of hatred in his eyes…cold, hard, soulless. She didn't want to give him a reason to act on that.

But, as soon as she made it to the box, she wished she hadn't. She wished she had stayed where she was. Hannah drew in a sharp, shocked breath, and wished he hadn't. The smell coming from the box had bile rushing up her throat. Her face paled at what she saw.

There, inside the box, was the crumpled body of a deer. Beneath it, a pool of dried, congealed blood had formed, and its eyes, once alive with energy and life, were glassy and empty.

She let out a groan of disgust and started gagging, wondering how long it had been in there. By the looks of it, it was starting to decay already.

"Get back here," Jed warned her, reaching in to the van and grabbing her ankle roughly, yanking her back toward the door.

She put her head down between her legs, feeling the bile twisting and burning in her throat.

Why did they have that here? Were they going to do the same to her? She couldn't believe this was happening. She had ignored her instincts about Jed too long. She would never let that happen again, not as long as she lived. *If* she lived. If there was someone who came into the lodge in the future who gave off a weird vibe, she would pay attention and tell one of the others immediately.

She hated how easy it had been for him to get close to her, to the other women, and it made her sick to think of how much danger they had been in without even knowing it. At least she had been the one he'd chosen. If it had been River, Hannah wasn't sure she would have been able to handle it, after everything else she had been through.

But could Hannah handle it? She had no idea. There was a part of her that wanted to take a chance and try to run to the woods and disappear. She wanted as far away from these vile men as she could get. But she knew she wouldn't get far, if any length at all, with her hands still bound and with the gun Jed now had pressed against her hip.

Her brain told her to wait it out, bide her time and see how things went down. It was really the only smart option in her current situation.

The man finished up his call, and then turned back to Jed. "Dutch'll be here soon. Get ready."

"Who's Dutch?" Hannah blurted before she could stop herself.

Finally, the other man turned in her direction, locking eyes with hers. The feel of his weighted gaze made her insides twist with dread, and she wished that she had kept her mouth shut.

The man reached out for her, and she tried to shrink away at once, but he grabbed her chin, forcing her to turn and face him. "He's the man you can blame for you being here in the first place," he replied. "He's the one who put you in this position. Wrong place, wrong time... Just bad luck, sweetheart."

"Don't call me that," she retorted defiantly.

But the man just smiled. "Oh, a bit of attitude, huh? I can see why Dutchy likes you. But it's not going to be enough to save you."

"Don't worry, not long now until you and Xavier will be together again," Jed told her, his voice mocking.

Xavier? That was who they were waiting for? Dutch was Xavier? Hannah was totally confused. She bit the inside of her cheek to keep from asking any more questions. She didn't want this man's attention on her any longer than necessary.

"You'll be all cozy like that deer in the back of the van," the other man added, stroking a hand down her hair. "Wrapped up in a tarp together. How about we bury you with one another? You'd like that, huh?"

Hannah's eyes shifted around to the box again and noticed a heavy blue tarp rolled up behind it against the back doors of the van. Her vision turned hazy, and she felt like she couldn't get enough oxygen. Xavier was walking into this thinking he was going to save her, but these evil men had always planned to kill them both no matter what. The nausea was starting to rise again. No...she couldn't lose him...

She was torn. She wanted him here with her, wanted him to be the last person she saw before she died, but not at the expense of himself. Not after he'd been working so hard to reclaim his life and his happiness. He didn't deserve that.

But at the same time, she wondered if he knew he was walking in to a trap. He'd have to know, though, right? The man was using her as bait to draw Xavier here, and he had to know that. She also knew that'd he'd come anyway; he'd try his damnedest to rescue her from these men. To end this nightmare for them once and for all. He'd do whatever it took to keep her safe.

Regret rolled through Hannah at the thought of losing Xavier before she'd had a chance to tell him how she felt. That she loved him. A sudden image popped into her head of Xavier in the same position as the deer, eyes glassy and blank and still as a board. She couldn't stop the bile from rising up her throat again.

She leaned over the edge of the van and threw up between her feet.

Jed jumped back in disgust, muttering a curse at her.

Her whole body shook violently and she was covered in sweat, but she was still frozen to the core at the thought of what these men were planning to do to them. It felt like such a sick, cruel joke. The two of them had come so far and finally had a chance at true happiness. For it to suddenly end like this, it just wasn't fair.

"Disgusting," the man tsked. "Keep an eye on her. I'm going to watch the road for Dutch."

Jed shot her a foul look. "You better not cause any more trouble, or I'll end you now," he snarled at her.

There was such hatred in his voice, she wondered for a moment how he could have hidden it behind a friendly façade for so many days. He was obviously a great actor to have been able to trick them all. Even if something felt off about him to the women, he hadn't raised any red flags around the men. It was clear from the way he looked at her that he had nothing but total and utter contempt for her.

Her mind was racing with questions—there were so many things she wanted to ask. But she knew to keep her mouth shut. She'd have a better chance of surviving this if she sat quietly and stayed alert to anything that might give her an advantage to escape.

Xavier was coming for her. She knew that now. He would never leave her out here alone with no help. Probably her brother, too. Lawson had always been overprotective of his baby sister, probably even more so now if she survived this. And he ran that tactical team out of the lodge, so the rest of the guys would be with them, too. These two men would be outnumbered and outmatched. They'd all show up to take them down.

As hard as it was for Hannah, she just had to be patient and wait. They'd already be on the way to find her. According to the other man, Xavier was en route. She just prayed they'd be safe, that no harm would come to any of her friends coming to rescue her. She couldn't bear the thought of them getting hurt because of her or having to face her girlfriends knowing she was the cause of their men being injured. She didn't want another mark of guilt on her conscience. It would take a while for the one for Jed to go away. If she'd just mentioned him earlier to Xavier or her brother...

She closed her eyes, drawing her knees up to her chest protectively. She didn't have any answers, only more questions that made her heart hurt. She supposed she was going to find out the answers soon enough, when Xavier and the others arrived.

They'd have a plan. They'd rescue her and take out the bad guys and everything would be good again. She couldn't let her mind go to darker places; she had to stay positive. They'd all make it out in one piece.

But as she sat there in the van in the middle of nowhere, she really didn't know for sure. And that scared her more than anything in the world.

# Chapter Twenty-Three

Xavier palmed the wheel, his phone propped up on the dashboard. Lawson's voice came through the speaker. Aside from feeling guilty about not listening to Hannah when she'd shared her concerns about Jed, Xavier also felt bad because he'd never shared any details with Lawson about Sampson before.

Lawson had cut him off when Xavier had tried to apologize and explain separately in a little more detail. He'd immediately said he understood. There had been a few times when Xavier and Lawson were at the agency that they had separate assignments with other agents. They both knew the rules: you didn't share details if it wasn't an operation you were directly involved with or had permission from the higher-ups to do so.

Xavier was positive that Lawson had several things he hadn't been able to share with him during their time at the agency and since. Even though neither of them was active any longer, they both knew to keep their mouths shut about assignments from their time there.

However, Xavier still felt terrible about it because his secret had brought dangerous men to their door and put Lawson's sister directly in harm's way. Xavier wasn't sure he'd be as forgiving if it had been the other way around.

He knew he'd never get over it if something happened to Hannah because of him.

"How far away are you?" Lawson demanded, bringing Xavier's thoughts back to their present situation.

"A few minutes," Xavier replied, trying to keep his voice steady, though all he wanted was to slam his foot down on the pedal and race to Hannah as quickly as he could.

It was hard to believe she had been taken, but Sampson was smart. He knew exactly what he needed to do to get Xavier to come to him. Thanks to Jed and his time at the lodge, Sampson knew Hannah was the one weakness he could use against Xavier to guarantee he'd come running. She was the one person he would protect at all costs, no questions asked.

Lawson let out a growl on the other end of the line. Xavier knew he was going through similar fear with Hannah being his baby sister. They both had everything to lose if this went sideways.

Xavier frowned. "You're sticking with our plan, right?" They were following behind, at a distance, in case Sampson and Jed had split up and one of them was watching the lodge. They'd wait a short time, then follow Xavier's general direction, but coming up on the other side through the forest instead of the road.

"Of course I am," Lawson muttered. "Wait until you get there, and then we'll all close in and cut them off so there's nowhere for them to go."

"Right," Xavier confirmed.

When Xavier had heard that Hannah had been taken, his first reaction was panic. He wanted to charge out to the location where Sampson was holding her and take them down in a fiery blaze, but Lawson had convinced him to wait. Make a plan and keep a level head.

He knew Lawson understood his urge to act. Of course he did, Hannah was his sister and he wanted her safe.

But Xavier knew Sampson too well to think he wouldn't follow through on his promise to kill her if they didn't play by his rules. If Lawson arrived before Xavier did, there would be hell to pay. Sampson would take her out before Xavier had a chance to do anything.

That thought had a sick feeling coursing through his stomach and made his headache pound more against his skull.

After he'd calmed down from the shock of Hannah being taken, Lawson had sent Xavier to his office to wait for River to come check him over. He'd grumbled slightly because they'd be wasting time but knew it was for the best. He wouldn't be any good to Hannah or himself if he couldn't even stand up straight.

Turned out Jed's beating had given him a slight concussion, several bruises and cuts over the top half of his body from that damn baton and had required sixteen stitches on the back of his head to close the wound. Xavier was achy and sore, and it felt like his brain was going to beat out of his skull, but he could see straight again.

While River was patching Xavier up, Lawson had called Cade to fill him in on everything and then gone to check on Sarah. Xavier felt horrible that her office had been trashed, too, and, more than anything, that she'd been traumatized. He was just glad she wasn't physically hurt. He would have never survived the guilt of that. Looked like he had a lot more therapy coming his way to get rid of all these new demons that had arisen.

Aaron had gone with Bailey, after she arrived with a team, to process the two destroyed rooms and get statements. She had left not long before they did to head back down to Blue Ridge to fill in Sheriff Willis and put out an APB on Jed and Sampson. Xavier was reluctant to let her do that, but if they happened to get away, hopefully they'd be caught by being flagged in the law enforcement system.

He still couldn't believe this had all happened. He should have done more to keep Hannah safe. He wished he would have locked down the whole damn place, if that would have protected her from these psychopaths. He should have dug deeper into Jed and asked him to leave the moment Hannah expressed any kind of doubt about him. But he hadn't. And now, his worst enemy had gotten his hands on her, and Xavier was all too aware of what Sampson would do to get what he wanted.

There was no USB drive anymore, but that didn't matter. Sampson was clearly crazed by the obsession of finding it. God only knew why he had chosen to come back now, but it didn't matter, Xavier would take him on. He was going to get Hannah away from him and make him pay for what he'd done—to her and to their home.

He was going to end this for good.

He pulled the car to a halt at the edge of a forestry road that led into the woods. It had been unused for years, but there was dirt kicked up around the edges like someone had been there recently. Sampson? Jed? He had to assume it was one of them. Climbing out of the car, he glanced around, making sure he wasn't being watched, but there was no one around him—no one he could see anyway. Good.

Above him, the nearly full moon hung in the sky, casting a bright light down through the trees. There was a stalled feeling in the air, like the forest was holding its breath waiting to see what would happen next. Xavier felt a bead of sweat running down his spine and the cold press of the gun tucked into his pants.

It had been a long time since he had carried a weapon, not since his days at the agency. It felt like a bad sign, like each step he took was carrying him closer and closer back to the life he left behind, full of secrets and lies and death and destruction. Goose bumps formed on his flesh at the thought of becoming what he'd been all those years ago.

But if that was what it took to get Hannah to safety—if he had to walk through hell to make sure she came out the other side of this—then he would do it. He had lost Max, and he refused to lose the person who had finally brought him out of the dark place he'd been trapped in for such a long time.

Lawson would never forgive Xavier if something happened to her, and he knew he would never be able to forgive himself, either. He wouldn't deserve forgiveness if something happened to her.

Leaves crunched beneath his feet, an eerie quiet filling the woods around him. His eyes scanned his surroundings as he tried to figure out where he was headed. Sampson had given him general directions but had kept it vague enough that they would have the jump on him if they wanted. He was going to do his best not to let that happen.

Suddenly, the sound of muffled voices caught his attention from deeper in the woods. He followed them, and a few moments later, he came to a clearing.

There, sitting in front of him, was the lifted Ford that

had forced him and Hannah off the road. He stepped around it, and then, with a flood of relief, he saw Hannah.

She gasped as soon as she laid eyes on him from where she sat in the open side of a van.

The moment the sound left her mouth, Sampson and Jed spun around to see exactly where he was. Jed grinned and grabbed Hannah, pulling her against him roughly. Even from where he was standing, Xavier could tell how terrified she was. Her face was drawn and pale and her whole body was stiff as Jed dragged her from the van and to her feet. She stumbled slightly at the jerking motion and her wide, scared eyes locked on Xavier's.

"It's going to be okay," Xavier told her, ignoring the other two as he lifted his hands up to show that he was unarmed. Well, as far as they knew anyway.

Sampson walked over and took Hannah by the collar of her shirt and yanked her forward. She stumbled behind him.

Xavier felt a flood of anger hit him, seeing them treat her like that. She was so sweet and sensitive in ways they would never be able to understand, and he loathed the way they dragged her about like she was nothing.

But he also knew she was fierce and brave and he was counting on that to keep her from panicking while he did what he needed to do. He didn't take his eyes off of her, silently pleading with her to believe him when he told her it was going to be all right, even though things seemed to have gone so wrong.

"Tell me where the drive is, Dutch," Sampson ordered, grinning at Xavier with a mad look in his eyes.

Xavier didn't know if he was stable enough to hear the truth of what he'd done all that time ago. Even though it had been so many years since he'd last seen the drive, Sampson still seemed to believe that Xavier was hiding it from him. He supposed Sampson was going to find out the truth sooner or later, whether he was ready or not.

Xavier took a breath, praying that what he said next didn't set Sampson off. "I don't have it."

A flash of anger crossed Sampson's face. "I know you do," he growled, jerking Hannah to a stop. "You were the last person who had it. Now, tell me where it is or—"

"I destroyed it," Xavier told him, keeping his voice as calm as he could. Lawson and the others would be on the way by now, and hopefully, they would catch up in time to help him. He just needed to keep Sampson talking long enough for them to get here.

Hannah bit down nervously on her lip, her eyes wide and laced with panic.

"You did what?" Sampson demanded. "You—"

"I destroyed it when we were on that last mission together," Xavier explained. "I was sure you were a rogue agent, and I couldn't trust you with it, so I made the executive decision to get rid of it. And it seems like I was right to do that, because look at you now."

The anger grew in Sampson's eyes. He shook his head like he couldn't believe what he was hearing. But on some level, he had to know it was true. Jed had turned Xavier's room upside down looking for the drive and hadn't been able to locate it.

"You were always too righteous for your own good," Sampson sneered. "If you don't have it, then you at least know where it is. Tell me."

"I just did," Xavier replied more forcefully. "I destroyed it. I don't have it. Nobody does. It doesn't exist anymore. I smashed it to pieces and then threw those pieces away years ago. It's probably scattered in some landfill somewhere now. You wouldn't be able to find it if you spent the rest of your life looking."

"That's too bad," Sampson replied, his voice taking on an almost unnerving tone of calm. He reached behind his back and pulled out a gun, training it on Xavier.

"No!" Hannah screamed, her voice cutting through the quiet woods around them.

Xavier stared down the barrel, not moving. If Sampson was going to shoot him, so be it. As long as the weapon wasn't pointed at Hannah, he could handle whatever came next.

But then, like he was reading Xavier's thoughts, Sampson turned to aim the gun at Hannah instead, taking his eyes off Xavier for a moment.

Big mistake. A flash of rage took over Xavier, and he grabbed his gun and pulled it out. By the time Jed had opened his mouth to warn Sampson what was happening, Xavier had managed to get off a shot. The bullet whizzed by Sampson's head and hit the van behind him.

Startled by the shot Xavier fired at him, Sampson dropped his gun and raced for cover behind the van.

Hannah rushed over to where Sampson's gun fell and kicked it farther away.

Jed took that moment to race behind the van for cover with Sampson, yelling obscenities at Xavier, leaving Hannah standing there alone. She was free.

*Hannah.* She was the only thing on Xavier's mind. Eyes fixed on her, he rushed toward her, the adrenaline pumping in his system, his heart slamming against his chest.

"Xavier!" she called out to him, her voice sounding strangely distant.

But then, all at once, he reached her and pulled her into his arms. And for a moment, everything fell into place.

## Chapter Twenty-Four

When Xavier pulled Hannah to him, she felt an instant wave of relief. She tried her hardest to keep the tears at bay, but they ran down her cheeks in waves. All she wanted to do was press further into Xavier's embrace and let everything else fade away. She knew they were still in danger but she couldn't seem to make herself move.

"Xavier. I was so scared." Her lips trembled as she mumbled into his shirt.

Xavier tightened his arms around her briefly, before setting her away from him. "I know and I'm sorry," he replied as he wiped the wetness from her face with his thumbs and looked around, noticed movement, and realized that Jed was making his way around to the other side of the van. He was going for Sampson. He and Hannah had to take cover now.

"We're not out of the woods yet, though. Come on."

Hannah looked around and realized Xavier was leading her to the other side of the truck for cover. She tripped, slightly off-center with her hands still bound.

"Quickly. Turn." He cut off her bindings so she'd be able to use her hands. She'd need them for balance and to help defend herself, if necessary.

As soon as her arms were loose, Hannah rubbed her

wrists and shook out her hands to help regain feeling. Then she turned her wide eyes on him, seeking reassurance and direction for what to do next. "Xavier," she breathed in relief. "What do—"

Before she could finish the sentence, he was pulling her farther behind the truck as Jed and Sampson ducked into the van across from them and started firing off rounds.

"Get down!" Xavier yelled out.

Hannah followed his order almost on autopilot. She was still trying to process everything that had just happened and that Xavier was actually here. He'd come for her and pulled her to relative safety. Seeing that gun pointed at him had sent a shock wave through her that she hadn't been ready for, pure horror at the thought of losing him.

"Make sure to stay behind this truck," Xavier instructed her as he pulled his gun out again, his back pressed against the door of the truck. "And stay down."

Hannah nodded. The way he was carrying himself and giving orders right now, she knew this was the former military version of him that had existed out in the field—back when he had lost his brother.

*Lost his brother.* When she realized that, how close this must feel to that fateful day, her eyes widened, and she wrapped her arms around her waist, hugging herself like she was trying to hold herself together. She hated that he had to relive a version of that again.

Bullets pinged off the front of the truck, making her jump, and she hugged herself tighter. She glanced over at Xavier as he peered out around the bumper and fired off a few shots in the direction of Sampson and Jed. The man she knew seemed to have vanished for a moment, replaced by this soldier, an agent who would do anything it took to bring his enemies down.

And it scared her. More than she thought it would.

She wasn't afraid of him. What frightened her was knowing he was back there again, in his darkest hours, even if they didn't have a choice. If they made it out of this alive, how would it affect him this time? Would he be able to recover from this or would it break him for good?

He ducked back behind the truck, catching his breath and reloading his gun with a clip from his pocket. He moved with a practiced swiftness that spoke of years of training and experience. If she hadn't been so scared, she would have been impressed at how well he was carrying himself, at how easy it seemed for him to slip back into this role once more.

But all she could see was the man she loved being stolen from her by a dark part of himself he had done his best to leave behind. She wondered if he even realized it in the moment.

A bullet ricocheted off the hood, and she jumped again and let out a small squeak.

"Stay down!" Xavier ordered her once more, his voice sounding hard and tinged with worry, not like his normal voice at all.

She squeezed her eyes shut, and he reached over to grab her arm.

"You need to stay alert," he told her. "Eyes open. Stay with me, Max."

*Max?* His brother's name. Her heart sank when she realized she'd lost him to his past. His mind was reliving that tragic day, pulling him out of their reality and thrusting him back to the day of his brother's death. Whatever was going on in his head right now, he wasn't seeing her or living in their current situation.

She wanted to call out to him, to try to pull him back to the present with her, but she wasn't sure how to do that or if she even had the time right now. They were in a precarious situation with bullets flying around them and two men who wanted them dead. Now didn't seem like the time for a distraction that could possibly get them killed.

All she knew for sure in this moment was that Xavier needed her here with him now. She wasn't going to let him down. She'd do whatever she could to help them both survive.

"You're only delaying the inevitable here. Just come out," Jed's mocking voice came from behind the van.

His words hardly seemed to register with Xavier as he turned to duck out from behind cover once more, lifting his gun and firing off a few more well-placed rounds.

Hannah clamped her hands over her ears, the loud noise hurting her. She'd never seen Xavier fire a weapon before. He seemed so disconnected...so focused and formidable. Not like the man she knew and loved, but more like who she assumed he used to be.

The change in him was worrisome, and she hoped with all her heart she'd be able to pull him back when it was all over.

Suddenly, Hannah heard voices closing in and saw lights cutting through the trees. Flashlights! Her heart skipped a beat. Others were here! Of course, he wouldn't have come all this way without backup.

"Hey!" Hannah yelled out. "Hey, we're here! And we need help!"

She continued to call out to whoever was coming,

hardly even caring who it was or if Jed and Sampson heard her. She needed someone else here, someone who could be on their side.

All at once, Aaron, Cade, and Lawson emerged in the clearing, guns drawn.

Hannah wanted to sob in relief. Lawson immediately locked eyes with her, and Hannah could tell from a single look just how relieved he was to see her. But then, his eyes slid to Xavier, and something in his face shifted. Obviously, he could see that something was seriously wrong with Xavier…something dangerous. He instantly became more tense, more focused, as if aware of the potential threat next to her.

The Xavier both of them knew and cared for so deeply had vanished, taken over by the man who'd been consumed by the darkness of his life before.

"Xavier!" Hannah called to him. "Help is here!"

He didn't seem to notice or care. He slipped out from behind the Ford once more, firing off a couple more shots toward Sampson and Jed where they were still shielded by the van.

She tried to reach for him, but when she touched his shoulder, he shrugged her off like it was nothing. He wasn't the man she knew right now, and she didn't know how to reach him. Several rapid-fire shots hit the front of the truck as Sampson and Jed returned fire.

Lawson and the others darted back to the edge of the trees for cover.

"Stay down," Xavier growled at her. He was still firing off orders like he was in the middle of a war zone. Lost to the past and the last battle where his brother had lost his life.

"Xavier, stand down!" Cade yelled to him.

For the first time, Xavier seemed to notice that there were other people here. He turned to face them, and Hannah saw in his cold, hard eyes that he perceived them as a new threat. He didn't recognize them. To his broken mind, they must look like enemies.

Hannah realized if she didn't think fast, he was going to do something awful and hurt someone he cared about. No amount of therapy would be able to bring him back from that.

Her mind raced with possibilities as to how she could help the man she loved right now. Shouting and gunfire were still all around them, and she knew that their friends would handle Sampson and Jed. Her primary concern needed to be Xavier, so she let everything else fade away.

She knew in that moment it wasn't just about them surviving these men, it was about getting Xavier back here in the present with her and their friends and realizing that they weren't the enemy.

While she was lost in thought trying to come up with a plan, she noticed that her brother had moved and was making his way toward them from the side.

"Xavier!" Lawson called to him.

Xavier immediately lifted his gun and aimed it at Hannah's brother.

Lawson stopped dead in his tracks, and Hannah's heart dropped.

"No! Xavier, he's not the enemy!" Her voice was filled with panic.

"What the hell are you doing?" Lawson asked Xavier, but Xavier didn't budge. He kept the gunned trained at Lawson's chest.

Hannah stood off to his side, but she felt as though she was a hundred miles away. She had to try something right now or she'd lose one or both of the men she loved more than anything. She took a deep breath and stepped closer to Xavier's side. With tears streaming down her face, she reached out and placed her hand on his chest right over his heart. She immediately felt his body go taut underneath her palm.

"Xavier," she spoke quietly in his ear. "Xavier, it's me, Hannah. I need you to come back to me."

He didn't acknowledge her, but she could feel a slight shift in him, his hand trembling on the gun aimed at her brother.

"Hannah, you need to step away. He can't hear you," Lawson told her, his voice rough with tension.

"Yes, he can. I know it," she breathed softly. With her hand over Xavier's heart, she could feel some of the tension easing in his muscles. She chanced a quick look up at his face and noticed some of the darkness leaving his gaze. He was coming back to her.

She stepped even closer, basically plastered to his side and tried again. "Please, please, come back to me. You're with me and our friends. You don't want to hurt anyone. Please."

"Hannah..." Lawson trailed off when she shook her head. Understanding she wasn't to be deterred, he heaved a large sigh and stood quietly, waiting.

Gunfire and yelling still surrounding them, she stepped directly in front of Xavier, took a deep breath, closed her eyes and planted her lips against his.

## Chapter Twenty-Five

Xavier knew it; backup wasn't going to make it in time. These enemies surrounding them, they were more than he and his brother could handle. His heart slammed against his ribs while his mind raced. He could feel the bite of the air against his skin, the sound of yelling around him, but it all felt louder than ever. The screaming in his ears was more than he could take.

If he hadn't come here, if he hadn't brought his brother here, they would both be safe. His blood rushed in his ears as he heard Max calling to him, telling him he was slow and needed to hurry his ass up. Even despite his words, Xavier could tell his brother was scared, trying to over-compensate with his cocky attitude.

If something went wrong, then it would all be his fault. There would be no way to take it back, it would be too late. He had to protect his little brother. He tightened his grip on his gun, ready to pull the trigger...

AND THEN HE FELT IT. The press of her lips against his. The taste of her salty tears on her skin.

For a moment, he had no idea what was happening, and his whole body started shaking as he came back to reality.

"Xavier," she begged him. "Please, Xavier. Tell me you're here with me. Tell me you're here."

Xavier blinked, and blinked again, trying to recall where he was. First, he registered Hannah's face. Beyond her was Lawson, fists and jaw clenched tight, staring at him with stormy eyes. Xavier looked down and realized he was holding a gun and pointing it at his best friend. Eyes wide, he clicked the safety and shoved the weapon back in his waistband.

Next, were all the noises, guns, shouting, fighting. Too much for his brain to process all at once. So he focused on the woman in front of him, letting everything else fade away. *Hannah.*

"It's okay, Hannah," he murmured to her. "I'm here. I'm back." He wrapped his arms around her and buried his face in her hair, inhaling her scent to ground him further.

"Oh thank God," she breathed as she caught his face in her hands. "I thought… I thought I had lost you." Tears streamed down her cheeks unchecked.

Xavier felt her shaking against him, but she was smiling. This wasn't like the day he had lost his brother; this was different. Backup had made it in time, and they were going to be okay.

He'd never had a flashback that intense while he'd been awake. Hannah's kidnapping and the gunfight must have triggered his mind in a way that forced him back to relive that horrible day when he lost Max. If it hadn't been for Hannah, something similar probably would have happened here. He might have killed his best friend.

He wrapped his arms around Hannah once more and kissed her forehead. "Thank you. You saved me."

Her face broke out in a grin, and she kissed his chin.

"And you saved me. I'm just glad you're back with us. With me."

"You okay?" Lawson asked him gruffly, clapping him on the shoulder as Xavier pulled back from Hannah.

"I'm sorry," he told his best friend. "I didn't see you…"

"I know," Lawson replied quickly. "But we need you to be here right now. With us. We're still fighting."

Xavier nodded again and reached for his gun. He handed it to Hannah. "Hold this," he told her. "I don't trust myself with it right now."

"Xavier, they can handle it—"

Xavier shook his head, cutting off her reply. She didn't understand. He had a job to finish. He could have hurt the woman he loved and had almost killed his best friend, her brother. This had to end, and he needed to be the one to do it. This was personal to him.

The first thing Xavier noticed as he rounded the hood of the truck was the quiet, no gunfire. The second was that Cade and Aaron had managed to sneak up on both Jed and Sampson, probably while they had been firing at Xavier. From what Xavier could see, Aaron had Jed handled. He was on the ground, face down, Aaron half-sitting, half-leaning on his back. Aaron had Jed's arms pulled back and was securing zip-ties around his wrists. Sampson, on the other hand, had managed to shove Cade to the side and was trying to make a run for it toward the woods.

Xavier quickly ran around the opposite side of the van to cut Sampson off, slamming into him and knocking him off his feet.

Sampson hit the ground on his back and rammed his knee up into Xavier's stomach as he came down over him.

"You really think you can stop me?" Sampson laughed in his face as he knocked Xavier to the side.

Xavier pushed back to his feet and rounded on Sampson has he pulled himself off the ground. "Just give it up," Xavier told him. "You're done. There's no drive, there's no *nothing*. You wasted your time on this for no reason, and now you're going to prison for it."

Sampson's eyes narrowed with anger, his face tight as he glowered at Xavier. He must have known Xavier was right. He could have gotten away with everything else he'd done if he had just forgotten about the drive. He was just too damn greedy.

And it was going to cost him everything.

Sampson launched himself at Xavier again, knocking him off his feet, and Xavier lifted his fist to drive it up into Sampson's jaw. Sampson's head snapped back, and blood dripped from his split lip as he turned back to Xavier. He swiped at the blood with his sleeve and charged again, diving for Xavier's legs.

As soon as Xavier's back hit the forest floor, he pushed off with his legs, flipping them over, with Sampson flat on the ground. They both pushed to their feet and charged, both swinging at the same time. Xavier's fist slammed in to Sampson's chin, drawing more blood, at the same time Sampson's arm went wide, hitting Xavier in the shoulder.

Both sprang back, circling each other and breathing hard. Xavier heard footsteps behind him, and Cade and Aaron appeared ready to take over.

"Xavier, let us—" Cade started.

Sampson took advantage of the distraction and charged Xavier again. He dodged out of the way just in time, leaving Sampson punching at air.

"I've got this!" Xavier yelled back at the two men, stopping them in their tracks. He had to be the one to bring an end to this, no matter what.

A few years ago, he might have been tempted to just let it go. But now, things were different. *He* was different. He had a woman he loved and who loved him back, and a life he wasn't going to give up without a fight.

Xavier flew at Sampson again, both landing hard on the dirt. Grappling around, Xavier finally got the upper hand and rolled on top of Sampson, grabbing Sampson's head with his hands and slamming it down into the hard earth.

Sampson let out a long groan and tried to scramble out from underneath Xavier, but Xavier had Sampson right where he wanted him.

He landed hit after hit, until there was no more fight left in him. Sampson lay there on the ground, blood leaking from his mouth and nose, eyes hazy with pain.

Xavier got to his feet, wiping the sweat from his brow and took a deep breath centering himself again. All at once they heard new voices echoing in the trees. Bailey and the other deputies were here. He stepped back and looked for Hannah, who was standing off to the side with Lawson, his arm wrapped around her like he was trying to hold her back.

Cade and Aaron rushed up to stand watch over Sampson, waiting for Bailey and the deputies with her to make their way down to them.

"Looks like we missed all the fun," Bailey quipped as she pulled out cuffs and slapped them on Sampson's wrists. Xavier looked to the side and noticed Jed being picked up off the ground by another deputy from where

Aaron had left him. Jed's face was bloody, too, so he and Aaron must have gone a few rounds before Aaron subdued him.

All at once, Xavier heard someone rushing toward him. He turned just in time to catch Hannah as she launched herself into his arms, wrapping herself around him and clinging on for dear life.

"Xavier!" Her cry was muffled from pressing her face into his neck.

He tightened his hold. "We're okay, Hannah. It's okay now." He pulled her back and kissed her forehead. He was still so angry he was vibrating with adrenaline at how horribly this all could have ended. But with Hannah safe and in his arms, the rage was starting to recede.

He pulled back slightly so he could gaze into her eyes for a moment. She was still so shaken, that much was obvious, but the first thing she had done was run to him for reassurance. She cared for him in a way nobody else ever had before.

She had seen the darkness in him, the battle he fought within, the part of him he kept hidden from his friends, and she hadn't run. She was still here, by his side and in his arms. She was brave enough to face his darkness and pull him back to the light. As long as she was by his side, he knew he would be okay.

"I'm so sorry," Hannah breathed. "I should never have let myself get taken. I should have—"

"It's okay," he murmured to her at once, smoothing a hand through her hair. "It's okay, Hannah, you have nothing to be sorry for. I should have done more to protect you. I should have listened to you when you said you had your doubts about Jed. I never should have let him get that close."

The two of them were talking over each other, spilling apologies faster than they could reply to them, until he kissed her again. She grasped him tight, like she was never going to let him go.

"We're safe," he promised her, planting a kiss against her temple. "I promise. We're safe."

She let out a long, shaky breath, but she seemed to believe him, managing to nod. With his arm around her waist, he steered her back toward the rest of the group.

"What happens now?" he asked Bailey.

"I'm passing this on to Willis," she explained. "With everything you gave him before, there's plenty to keep them locked up for now. And when you tell him the rest of the story, along with the damage to the lodge, what they did to Sarah and Hannah's kidnapping, the two of them are going to go away for a long, long time."

Xavier nodded slowly, taking the words in as she spoke. It almost felt too good to be true. This was it, he realized. The danger was gone. This was the last threat that had been pressing down on him for all this time. Now he could truly leave the past behind. Move on with the rest of his life and his future with the woman he loved.

"That sounds good. Thanks, Bailey."

"No problem, Xavier. We'll get these guys back to town and I'll tell Willis to contact you all at the lodge for statements later.

The sun was just starting to rise, and some of the light was beginning to filter through the trees. Hannah slipped her hand into his and squeezed it tight, seeming to need reassurance that he was right there with her and not sliding off into the nightmares that had plagued him for so long.

"You okay?" she asked him.

He nodded. It wasn't entirely true, but it was the closest he could come to the truth right now. He might not be all right in that moment, but for the first time in a long time, he knew he would be.

"We should get out of here," he told her, and she sighed in agreement, laying her head on his shoulder for a moment.

"Definitely," she agreed. "I want a hot shower. And a warm bed. And a huge meal. Not necessarily in that order."

He chuckled, already feeling some of the tension leaving his system. What was it about her that made everything easier, even a nightmare like this? Her softness, her kindness, her willingness to see the man beneath all the trauma and pain he had been through, beyond all the nightmares and horrors. She saw the person he wanted to be, the potential for who he could be, and it only made him even more certain that he would do everything he could to bring that man to life for her. Anything, as long as it meant they could be together and as long as he could make her happy.

The two of them followed the group out of the forest and into the sunlight beyond.

It was already shaping up to be another beautiful spring day.

## Chapter Twenty-Six

"I really can't apologize enough," Xavier told Sarah for what had to be the hundredth time since their appointment had started.

She smiled at him kindly, shaking her head. "You have nothing to apologize for," she reminded him.

The two of them were meeting in her temporary office space while her original office was being repaired from all the destruction Jed had caused. In his fit of rage, Jed had pretty much torn apart the entire room, so it would be a while before she could feasibly work from that space again. She had too many patients needing help to take time off, and she had insisted on moving to a makeshift office in another part of the building and starting up her appointments again as normal.

Xavier was grateful for that. It had been nearly ten days since Jed had attacked him and taken Hannah, and he still felt unsettled sometimes. Being there in the middle of that shootout and feeling himself drawn back to all of the memories he had tried to leave behind was scary as hell.

Losing himself completely, forgetting where he was, not even being able to recognize his friends and allies—he never wanted that to happen again. So he was taking all the steps he could to help ensure he never lost himself to his past life again.

"We all made it out in one piece," Sarah reminded him. "That's what matters most."

"Yeah, we got lucky," Xavier agreed. "Though sometimes I can't help but think about how horribly wrong it all could have turned out."

"And how do you feel about the fact that it didn't turn out badly?" Sarah asked, gently steering the conversation back around to the focus of their appointment.

"I feel…grateful," he replied finally, letting out a long breath. "Extremely grateful that I didn't lose Hannah or anyone else. I don't think I could have survived it if I had. The guilt of harming one of my friends would have been it for me."

"Well, grateful is a great place to start. A good emotion to focus on," she agreed, jotting something down. "Has it brought up anything else you're struggling with right now?"

"I… When I was out there," he confessed. "In the middle of it, it was like my memories…fractured. Like everything that happened with Max was spilling over into the present moment, and I couldn't tell the difference between what had happened in the past and what was happening right in that moment."

Sarah nodded and wrote something else down on her pad. "The mind is a powerful thing. And sometimes, when we're reminded of those moments that have stayed in our memory, it can feel like they're happening all over again. It's the brain's way of trying to protect itself. You didn't want to have to face the possibility of losing the woman you love, so your brain put in place the memories that you'd already started to deal with."

"Makes sense," he agreed. He was still trying to wrap his head around the way all of this worked. He had spent so long avoiding these conversations, actually accepting this help was still foreign to him, but the more he learned, the clearer all of this became. Instead of being stuck under the control of the nightmares he'd had for so long, he could look at them a little more objectively and deal with them more clearly than he had before.

"And what about the dreams?" Sarah asked him. "I would expect you've been dealing with some of them lately."

"I have been dreaming about my brother," he admitted. "But not the same flashbacks I'd been having before. The ones from the last time I saw him alive."

"No?" she prompted him, sounding interested.

"I had this dream about the two of us racing across the field behind our house when we were young," he said, feeling a smile spread over his face. "To see who would make it to the edge of the woods first." Xavier briefly closed his eyes, pulling up the memory again. "It was so long ago, I'd almost forgotten we used to do that. And I always gave him a head start, but he still accused me of cheating, even though I mostly let him win." He smiled and shrugged, looking a little sheepish. "I didn't want to deal with him whining about how I cheated." He chuckled at the thought. "Max was always a sore loser. And slow, for the record. He never actually beat me."

Sarah laughed. "It's great that you're finally able to talk about your happier memories with your brother. And even better that you're not having the dreams about his passing anymore."

"You think so?" Xavier asked. Some part of him had felt guilty about the dreams turning from painful to happy, as though he should have had to contend with his failure to keep his brother safe a little longer.

"I know so," she replied.

"Why do you think it's happened? It seems wrong in some way that I've gone from reliving his death to memories of our childhood," he asked, frowning. He'd only just started therapy again. It seemed too soon to have made such huge steps forward and for his feelings of failure to suddenly be gone.

"I can't tell you the exact reason," she remarked. "But I can give you my theory, if you want."

"Go ahead," he replied, gesturing for her to keep talking.

"You've struggled for a long time feeling like you failed your brother," she explained. "Even though there was nothing more you could have done to help him. But now, this time, you saved *her*. And I think your mind knows on some level that he would be proud of you for that. Proud of both of you, actually. You're starting to forgive yourself, because this time, it went differently."

Xavier paused, taking it all in. It sounded right to him. His mind accepted that explanation. He hadn't been able to save Max, no matter how much he had wanted to, but he had been able to save Hannah. And maybe that was enough to start the process of forgiving himself. And letting him find some peace.

THAT EVENING, HANNAH snuggled next to Xavier on one of the couches in front of the fireplace in the lodge's reception area. They had all decided on gathering in this room to warm themselves up after a long day of work putting the lodge back together. Sarah's office was the main focus, but Hannah and River had been out planting some more flowers, too. Her hands were still chilly as she pushed them into Xavier's and rested her head on his shoulder. Even though the spring days were warm, it still got chilly at night. Perfect for snuggling by the fire.

Opposite them, the rest of the space was filled with their friends—Cade and River, Bailey and Aaron, and Sarah and Lawson, wineglasses in hand and a quiet peace resting over all of them. After the chaos of the last several months, there was something distinctly precious about this time they had together, without having to look over their shoulders and worry about what was going to happen next.

As the season changed from winter to spring before their eyes, Xavier's mind had drifted to the future, too. There was so much he wanted to do, so much he wanted to try. Now that some of the weight of his past had been lifted off his shoulders, it felt like he could see a whole new future, something he had never let himself imagine before.

"Those flowers are already starting to bloom, Hannah," Bailey remarked as she peered out of the window beside her. "They're looking gorgeous. I can't wait to see how they'll look when summer comes."

"Yeah, everything looks better in summer," Aaron agreed, shooting Xavier a conspiratorial grin. He knew what Aaron was planning, because he had had come to Xavier to ask for help picking out the ring. He could have gone to Hannah, but he was worried she might spill the beans to Bailey before he was ready, and he wanted it to come as a complete surprise. Xavier knew Aaron could hardly wait to see the look on her face.

"Good time for a wedding, too," Aaron added as casually as he could.

Hannah frowned. "What do you mean, a wedding?"

Bailey's lips parted in surprise, but before she could say anything else, Aaron handed his wine over to Xavier and dropped to one knee in front of Bailey.

Hannah's hand flew to her mouth, and River spluttered into her drink in shock.

"Bailey, our paths to each other haven't always been easy," Aaron began as he reached into his pocket to pull out a ring. "But all that matters to me is that our path to our future is one we embark on together." He popped open the box, showing off a glittering band with an oval-shaped diamond planted in the center.

Bailey's eyes nearly bugged out of her head.

"Will you marry me, Bailey?"

"Yes! Of course I will!" she exclaimed, almost dropping her wine as she sprang to her feet.

Aaron laughed and stood up to meet her, planting his lips against hers and pulling her into a warm embrace.

Hannah squeezed Xavier's hand gently as they watched the scene unfold in front of them, two of their friends dedicating themselves to one another.

"Now get that damn ring on my finger already," Bailey ordered him, and everyone laughed as he slipped the sparkly ring onto her finger. She gazed at it for a moment and then back to him, sinking into his arms again.

The rest of the evening was spent celebrating the newly engaged couple. Sarah went to the kitchen to dig out a bottle of champagne, and they shared it as they toasted to Aaron and Bailey's future happiness. It was a perfect evening, the antidote to everything they had been through with Sampson less than two weeks prior.

It was these nights at the lodge that Xavier lived for, surrounded by his friends, knowing he was safe…they all were safe…and there was nothing for him to worry about or fear any longer.

By the time the champagne was gone, he could tell Hannah was starting to get a little tipsy, and he led her outside so they could head back to their cabin. The two of them were living together now, as if he could spend a moment apart from her.

Even if his room hadn't been trashed, he would have wanted to wake up next to her every day. Their little coffee dates every morning gave him a reason to get out of bed, and eating dinner together at their tiny kitchen table was the perfect way to end each day. He couldn't ask for anything more.

He pulled her into his arms and planted his lips against hers in the cool evening air.

She giggled and smiled up at him, gazing at him with those beautiful eyes that still set his heart pounding in his chest. As he stared down at her, she cocked an eyebrow at him.

"Don't tell me that proposal has you feeling all romantic," she teased him.

"It's not that," he replied. "Just you."

He kissed her again, brushing his thumb over her cheek and pausing to take this moment in. There had been so many times where he had felt as though he would never feel true happiness again. Never be rid of the guilt weighing him down or the nightmares about his brother. But when he was with Hannah, it all seemed to fade away. He could just be there in the present with her.

He knew there was still a lot of work to be done when it came to healing himself entirely. But this? This was the start he needed. The reason he needed to keep going. To become the man she wanted him to be, the kind of man she could spend her life with. He would work every day of his life to make sure he got there.

"But there is something I want to tell you," he murmured. "Something I should have said a long time ago." He paused, looking down into her expectant eyes with a smile on his face. He wanted to linger in this moment forever. There were so many memories in his mind that he wished he could escape, but when he was with her, none of them seemed to matter. The only thing he cared about was her, and he wanted her to know just how deep his feelings for her ran.

She pushed her fingers into his hair, hand tracing the nape of his neck. He was sure she could tell what was on his mind. The two of them had felt this way about each other for so long now, but they hadn't actually spoken the words out loud yet. He needed her to hear it from him. Needed her to know.

"I love you," he told her softly, the words feeling right escaping his lips.

She smiled, that beautiful smile that seemed to light up the whole world around her, and stood on her tiptoes to plant her lips against his.

"I love you, too," she replied. "Now, let's get back to the cabin before I freeze out here."

"Hmm, I can think of a few ways to keep you warm," he remarked playfully, and she giggled.

"I bet you can," she replied. "Why don't you come show me?"

Taking his hand, she led him down the path toward their cabin, the flowers along the path just starting to come into bloom. Just like their love.

# *Epilogue*

Hannah shivered as she stood next to the cold plunge tub. Why had she agreed to this again?

"You ready?" Xavier asked as he stood next to her in his swim trunks. The sight of him almost undressed was enough motivation to get her out of bed this early in the morning, but she wasn't sure anything could convince her to get into that water.

"No," she replied, and she reached out to slip her fingers into the tub. She snatched her hand back at once, letting out a cry. "Oh my God, it's so cold!" she protested. "You sure I can't just go have my morning coffee instead?"

"No, you promised," he reminded her, raising his eyebrows pointedly. "We have to test this out before any of the guests try it, right?"

"Right," she muttered, grimacing as she imagined submerging her whole body under the freezing water. "Tell me what it's supposed to help with again?"

"Reduces inflammation, increases circulation, improves metabolism and mood," he replied, ticking off the benefits on his fingers. He grinned at her. "You ready now?"

"Ugh, I guess so," she muttered, as she dropped the

robe she had been hanging on to for dear life. She was in her one-piece swimsuit, and the warm summer that was starting to come in wasn't enough to keep her from shivering.

"You'll feel so good when you're out, I promise," he told her, grabbing her hand and helping her up the wooden steps to the tub.

"Three, two, one…" Xavier announced, and then the two of them both leaped into the water.

"Oh my God, no, no, no!" Hannah shrieked as soon as the freezing water hit her body. "No way!"

"It's not that bad," Xavier replied, but his teeth were already starting to chatter.

She laughed, even as the cold started to set in around her. "Yes, it is!" she protested. She was well aware that they were probably going to get into trouble for causing such a racket this early in the morning, but she didn't care. She curled her toes and tried to breathe, her body already crying at her to get out. It went completely against every part of her nature to sit here in freezing water. For goodness' sake, it went against human nature! She should have been stepping out of a hot shower right now, preparing a warm cup of coffee, not freezing her butt off in this tub.

"I bet I can last longer than you," he told her, and she narrowed her eyes at him. If he thought it was going to be that easy to beat her, he was wrong.

"Oh, yeah?" she replied, wrapping her arms around herself beneath the water. "Let's find out, huh?"

He knew there was no better way to get her to do something than to suggest she couldn't. She was stubborn right down to her bones. And she wasn't going anywhere.

"You can get out anytime you like," he teased her, even as his words started to shake from the cold.

"Oh yeah, so can you," she shot back. "You all right over there? Looks like you're struggling."

"I feel great," he replied, but he forced the words out through gritted teeth. His whole body was covered in goose bumps, and he was already glancing toward the spot where he had left his robe.

"Do you, now?" she asked him, nudging him with her foot under the water. "It's really cold in here. Nobody would blame you if you had to—"

But she couldn't even get the words out before he sprang from the water and grabbed his robe, wrapping it around himself quickly.

"Damn, that's cold!" he cried out, and she laughed and kicked her legs beneath the water.

"Really?" she replied, feigning innocence and trying to keep her own teeth from chattering. "I think it's just lovely in here." She counted out another ten seconds but then climbed out of the water, shivering wildly and slipping on her robe. "You know what, beating you really did improve my mood," she remarked as she reached for her shoes. "Maybe there's something to all of this after all."

"I should have known not to challenge you," he muttered, chuckling. "You never let yourself get beat."

"Exactly," she agreed, as she crouched down to slip on her flip-flops. These last few months had been some of the best of her life, partly because she had realized a strength in herself she had never noticed before.

She had started therapy at Xavier's request, after what she had been through at the hands of Jed and Sampson. She had been so focused on helping Xavier get back on his feet, she had found herself kept up late with nightmares and memories of her own.

Focusing on herself in therapy made all the difference, and she'd found herself better able to handle those dreams when they came around. As time passed, they were becoming less frequent and ferocious, and she knew it wouldn't be long until they all but vanished entirely.

It helped, of course, that Sampson and Jed had been locked up with the key pretty much thrown away. No court date had been set yet, as the state pulled together all of the evidence it needed to get them put away for life, but it was clear they weren't going to be getting out anytime soon. The horrors they had put her through, and the hardships they had caused for Xavier, were well and truly a thing of the past.

She hoped they would stay there, though she was sure she would have to testify against them when the case eventually went to trial. One of the reasons she was so determined to see her therapy through was so she'd be strong enough in her testimony to ensure they got a life sentence.

Seeing how much it had helped Xavier had also convinced her it was the right thing for her. It seemed nothing short of a miracle to Hannah that he had changed so much in these last few months, and she knew Sarah was a big part of that.

He had put in so much work, learning all these techniques to ground himself and pull himself out of a flashback when one hit him. She could only imagine how tough it had been to relive all those memories again in order to work through them.

But the person she had seen in the woods on that

fateful day, she never laid eyes on again. The man who seemed so lost to his memories, to the bad dreams and his past, was gone now. When she looked at him, she saw his softness, his kindness—his dedication to making sure that nobody had to suffer the same way he had.

He had been an amazing support as she got back on her feet after the attack, and to the guests at the lodge, too. He understood so well what a lot of them had been through, and he did whatever he could to help them through it, encouraging them to get therapy and able to tell them exactly how it had helped him. His strength and kindness never failed to amaze her, and she was so proud to be able to call such a good man hers.

He talked a lot about his brother these days, which was such a nice change from before. For so long, he had hardly spoken Max's name out loud, but now, it was different. The happy memories he shared with her made her wish that she'd had a chance to know Max properly, but at least she could get to know him through his proud older brother's memories. That was something.

She had put up a picture of Max and Xavier as kids in their cabin, one that she'd dug up from his old room. It wasn't much, but it was some kind of reminder of him, of their happy times together.

She had never been happier, not in her whole life. Helping Bailey organize her wedding, coming up with fun wedding favors with River, watching the flowers she had planted bloom over the course of the summer, sharing the evenings with all of her friends, including her brother, who was totally accepting of her relationship with Xavier. It was everything she could have asked for, everything she could have dreamed of, and she wouldn't have changed a thing.

Well, maybe one thing. As she dried herself off, she pulled a face as she looked down at the flip-flops she'd brought with her.

"What's wrong?" Xavier asked, noticing her annoyance.

"Those things gave me blisters on the way out here," she complained. "It's going to hurt like hell getting back to the cabin to warm up. I should have brought something else with me."

"Well, maybe you can next time," he suggested.

She laughed. "Oh, you want a rematch already, huh?" she asked, pretending to square up to him.

He grinned and put his arms around her. "How about I carry you back?" he suggested.

She smiled, leaning into him. "I guess I could manage that," she agreed, and he swooped her up into his arms. "When did you become such a romantic?" she asked, and he lowered his mouth to hers.

For a moment, she forgot all about the bet he'd made and the fact she'd won. When he kissed her like that, nothing else in the world mattered to her.

"When I realized I could drop you back in the cold plunge tub," he murmured.

Her eyes widened. "Wait, what?"

But before she could get another word out, he dropped her back in the water—robe and all—and took off running.

"You're *so* dead!" she yelled after him, but she was laughing so much she could hardly get the words out. The freezing water rushed through her again, and she scrambled out as fast as she could. She took off her soaked robe and fished her flip-flops out of the water, then took off after him. She didn't care who saw her as she sprinted in the direction he had gone, robe and shoes in hand.

She saw him vanish down the path into the woods, just past the row of flowers she had planted before the first frost the year before. She put on a burst of speed, rushing to catch up with him, laughing so hard she could barely catch her breath.

When she finally caught up to him, he was already back at their cabin, sitting on the porch swing with a triumphant grin on his face.

"What took you so long?" he asked as nonchalantly as he could while still trying to catch his breath.

She matched his tone, stepping onto the porch. "Oh, I was just doing a little extra cold plunging. It has a lot of health benefits, you know."

"Does it?" He raised his eyebrows.

"Sure does. It reduces inflammation, increases circulation, improves metabolism and mood... I'm pretty much a champ at it."

He threw his head back and laughed. "Okay, champ, what do you say we warm up together in a hot shower? I hear that can have a few health benefits, too."

Hannah agreed enthusiastically, and as she followed him into their cabin, she realized that she was living her dream. She was safe, she was loved, and she was so incredibly happy.

She couldn't ask for anything more.

* * * * *

# Get up to 4 Free Books!

**We'll send you 2 free books from each series you try PLUS a free Mystery Gift.**

FREE Value Over $25

Both the **Harlequin Intrigue®** and **Harlequin® Romantic Suspense** series feature compelling novels filled with heart-racing action-packed romance that will keep you on the edge of your seat.